FEELING THE FIREWORKS

For my daughter Aurora, the best reason for this book taking longer than planned.

CHAPTER ONE

It was the same old routine, the same old commute, the same luke-warm coffee that Elizabeth Davis had every morning. She tried not to contemplate how little had changed in her life over the last few years, but sometimes - like today, when she was stuck in traffic trying to get into the centre of Exeter, having left a little too late (as usual) - it was hard to not let her mind wander.

She had once thought she was the daredevil of the family: the one who would stay up all night drinking at a moment's notice; the one who went through jobs and men at a rate of knots; the one who didn't feel the need to have her life mapped out in front of her.

And then she found herself stuck in a rut. Keeping the same job, because even though it was going nowhere, she had rent and bills to pay - and was sick of having to run to her mum or her sister for a bailout. Feeling too tired for those all night drinking sessions, because the early starts took their toll. Well, that and the fact that, at twenty-eight, most of her friends were no longer in the let's-do-tequila-shots-till-4am phase of their lives. No, they had steady boyfriends (something Beth had little experience of), or husbands, or children, or even *mortgages.*

"Get over onto your side!" she screamed at a lorry that had swerved far too close to her lane for comfort - but the distraction did at least stop her mulling over her life - for a few moments, at least. She waved at the security guard as she parked in the little car park that was attached to the printing firm she'd been at for the last two years. She always wondered why on earth they needed a security guard - nothing exciting ever happened at Chilster and co.

She'd started on an internship, even though she'd been way too old to be an intern, really, when she'd thought she might be interested in a career in publishing. That had fizzled out by the second month, but she - and they - had realised that she made a pretty good secretary, and so when a maternity role had come up, she'd been the obvious candidate. Then when it became permanent...well, it paid the bills. It definitely was not her passion; it definitely was not a career that she thought she would be pursuing for the rest of her life - but Beth had long ago come to the conclusion that she was not one for life plans and long term goals.

Her sister, on the other hand, always had been. Beth supposed that was what always made her feel like a rebel - her older sister Shirley (who was not quite as old as the name suggested, and went by Lee) had *always* been the good one. She'd gone to university, got a career in law, got married, bought a house, got made a partner by the time she was thirty... everything their mother, with her habit of naming her daughters as if they were already in their seventies, had ever wanted.

And then...

And then Lee's seemingly perfect life had been ripped to shreds by her cheating husband, and before Beth knew it, she was no longer the rebel of the family. Oh no, Lee left her home, her job, moved to the middle of nowhere in Devon, bought a café… the list of shocking events was endless. Then there was the fact that Lee had met a drop dead gorgeous police officer, had a child with him and was currently engaged!

It had certainly been a whirlwind year in the Davis family - and it put Beth's life rather into perspective.

"Morning Beth!" called Jasmine, the latest intern. At 23, she was a few years younger than Beth, but Beth found they had a lot in common - certainly more than she did with the thirty- and forty-year-old publishers that she generally worked with.

"Lunch out today?" Beth called over, dumping her bag on her desk and accidentally knocking a few errant paperclips off the table as she did so.

Jasmine gave her a thumbs up, and Beth smiled to herself at the glare they both got from Victoria, the ancient (or at least she seemed it to Beth) head of accounts. Jasmine and Beth's high energy never seemed to go down that well at work… but then, to be fair, the energy was quite often directed away from their actual workloads, and towards things like where and when to have lunch, or whether they could make it to the shops to look round the sales before they closed.

The smile dropped off her face fairly rapidly as she turned on her computer and was faced with a surprisingly full inbox. The mundane task of wading through and clearing emails - some of which were trying to get her buy something, some of which were authors trying to get their work seen, some of which were just spam - signalled the start of yet another morning in a job which, she had to admit, wasn't going anywhere.

❖ ❖ ❖

Lunch with Jasmine was, as usual, the highlight of her day. They had discussed the guy Jasmine was currently seeing - an IT technician from two doors up - and how he wanted to introduce her to his mother.

"I don't do meeting the parents," Jasmine said, rolling her eyes and tossing her raven-black hair across one shoulder dramatically. "Never have done."

"You're only twenty-three!" Beth reminded her with a laugh. "But I get you, I've never been the meet-the-parents type either."

"Besides, I'm hardly going to introduce him to my parents. They'll freak out if they find out I'm dating someone who's not Indian, you know what they're like-" Beth had never met them, but Jasmine had complained about them and their puritanical views enough that she felt as though she did. "I'm not crossing that bridge unless it's someone I'm going to spend the rest of my life with."

"And I take it you don't think Joe is?"

"No..." she said, gazing off into the distance as she often did. "No, I don't think he is. He's great for now, though..." she said, with a dirty laugh that had Beth laughing along with her.

"And what about you?" Jasmine asked, turning her eyes back on Beth. "How's things with what's-his-name?"

"Dean? Over before it started, if I'm honest..."

"What happened?"

"Nothing major, no big drama to report, I'm afraid! He asked me out, we went to a nice bar, saw him again for dinner last Thursday, he asked me back to his..."

Jasmine wiggled her eyebrows suggestively and Beth giggled.

"But the spark just wasn't there..."

"You don't need fireworks with every guy!" Jasmine said, sipping her coffee as she checked her watch. Five minutes 'til they needed to head back to the office.

"I'm not wasting time and energy on somebody with no fireworks, Jas - too old for that nonsense!"

"Pfft, not that old!"

"Not that far off thirty, I'm afraid to say - and my sister's nearly married again with a kid!"

"Do you want a kid, now, really?"

"Well, no, obviously..."

"Stop whining then and live life while you're young, free and single. Let's go out, Saturday night - you and me. I bet we can find you some fireworks..."

By six, Beth was home in her little flat, with its mismatched pillows and throws and last night's plate (and wine glass!) still sitting on the side. It was quiet, as it always was, and she dumped her bag and coat, as well as a bag of food shopping she'd picked up on her way home, onto the kitchen counter. Lunch with Jasmine always lifted her spirits, but coming home to a silent, empty flat and dinner for one brought them right back down again.

Luckily, her phone rang before she could get too down in the doldrums again, and a smile lit up her face as she saw her sister's name on the screen.

"Shirley!" she answered with a grin, as her sister threw some abuse down the line for using her given name. "I hope my favourite niece can't hear those terrible words you're calling her aunty!"

"Well don't call me Shirley then, *Elizabeth*," Lee retorted.

"How are you sis?"

"All good here," Lee said. "Exhausted, Holly seems to have stopped sleeping through the night again... apparently not that uncommon at 8 months, but just when I thought we were getting somewhere..."

"Is James doing his fair share?"

She could hear her sister smiling through the phone. "Yeah, he's up at least as much as I am, even though he's the one working full time..." Lee's fiancé and the father of her baby, James, was a police officer in rural Devon - and Beth was fairly sure the uniform had been one of the things that first caught Lee's eye.

"How's the café?"

"It's doing great actually - I've started doing a day a week, just to get myself back into it, but what with the law work I'm taking on too, I have to admit I'm not in there as much as I like. Gina runs it amazingly though, so I don't need to worry!"

"Don't work yourself too hard - you don't want to burn out!"

"I'm good Beth, promise. And how's things with you? How's the job?"

"Eh," Beth said, unable to hide her apathy. "It's a job. Pays the bills..."

"Have you got any holiday due?" Lee asked. "You know we'd love to see you - the weather's nice, we could go to the beach, take Holly - and June's the best time really, before the kids break up from school and the grockles invade for the season."

"Grockles?!" Beth asked with a laugh.

"Sorry, sorry, the Devon lingo gets to you in the end. Tourists!"

"Well I'll be one of those tourists, won't I! But that does sound great... let me check with work, and get back to you, okay?"

"You're always welcome Beth - say the word, the spare room's yours."

Beth felt a flash of guilt - she really ought to visit her sister more, she knew. Whenever they did spend time together it was so great - but they were both busy, and it was easy for weeks or even months to pass by without meeting in person.

"I promise, I'll come down soon - the beaches are calling to me!"

CHAPTER TWO

The week passed by in a hot blur, with most of her work conversations revolving around the unusually warm and dry weather they were having, and whether there was a maximum temperature the office could be before they had to be sent home (it turned out there wasn't).

After work on Friday, before even heading up to her flat, she decided it was far too nice to be stuck indoors. She headed out along the river, wandering the well-worn footpath and jumping out of the way for cyclists that beeped their horns every now and again for her to move out of the way, without any real purpose to her meandering.

She watched as a couple sat on a bench, sharing a sandwich and looking out over the river; a young woman sat curled up on the next bench with a well-worn novel, and Beth let her mind wander to the last time she'd read a book. As a kid she'd devoured novels, but of late she couldn't bring herself to start one, even with plenty of long evenings by herself.

Making a promise to herself to head to a bookshop in the near future, she head for home, making a stop along the way for a nice cold bottle of wine.

◆ ◆ ◆

Saturday evening rolled round just as balmy, and after a day spent lazing around the house and not getting enough housework done, Beth was looking forward to a night on the town with Jasmine. Nights out had definitely become less regular, and she relished the chance to get dressed up, put some make up on and drink a few - or more! - glasses of wine.

They'd arranged to meet at eight, and it was almost ten to by the time Beth stepped into her taxi, wearing a fail-safe little black dress and gold heels that caught the sun as much as her blonde hair. She had always been quite petite, and the heels made her feel a little more powerful out in the wide world.

Jasmine was late, as usual, and Beth sat on a bench outside the bar, looking over the river, thinking not about their evening but about her upcoming trip to Devon. Work seemed happy enough for her to take the holiday she was owed in a little over a week's time - which Beth found depressed her a little. After all, if they didn't need more notice or time to find someone to cover, how useful could she really be?

Luckily, Jasmine bounced into view, wearing a killer gold dress with heels to match, derailing Beth's thoughts from their miserable path.

"They're not going to know what's hit them!" Jasmine said in way of greeting, glancing over Beth's outfit. "There better be some fireworks tonight!"

"What about you?!" Beth said with a laugh. "You're in a

relationship, remember?"

"Doesn't mean I can't make an effort! I dress like this for me, not for the men who might happen to see me!"

◆ ◆ ◆

Three glasses of wine and two shots later, Beth was not feeling quite so cheerful.

"What am I doing, Jas? With my life?"

"I have no idea. What am I doing with mine?"

"But you're five years younger than me!" Beth hiccuped as she spoke. "I'm on the path to *nowhere*."

"That's not true! You've got a job-"

"That probably wouldn't replace me if I got hit by a bus tomorrow."

"And a flat!"

"That's a mess! And is rented, so they could kick me out any time they like."

"You've got family-"

"Now you're clutching at straws. They don't live near, and besides, I need something in my life that's not my mother or my older sister. They've got their own lives!"

Jasmine sat, silenced, looking a little stumped.

Beth groaned, and lay her head on the table - before immediately regretting it when she realised it was slightly sticky. "You know I'm right. No career, no proper home, no serious relationship on the horizon... before you know it, I'll be five years older and be in exactly the same situation."

"Would that be awful?" Jas asked, sipping some bright pink cocktail.

"I think it would. I think I need... something."

"A man."

"No, not necessarily a man! Something else in my life, other than all this!"

"Charming," Jas said with a sniff.

"Oh you know what I mean! But at some point your internship will come to an end, and you'll leave me for some hotshot career, and I'll still be here, thirty-odd by that point and still alone, and still with no real goal, or passion, or..."

"Something," Jasmine supplied, not too helpfully.

"Something."

"Tonight was supposed to be fun!" Jasmine said, prodding her friend in the arm. "Not being drunk and miserable. We were meant to be finding you fireworks!"

"I'm not sure they exist anymore... I can't remember the last time I felt true fireworks," Beth replied.

"No. We are not spending the whole evening like this. Just because I can't hook up with random strangers does not mean the same is true for you. You are not over the hill, Beth - you are twenty-eight years young. Come on, no arguments."

There definitely were arguments, but Jasmine was deaf

to them, and dragged Beth onto the dance floor and into the pathway of a group of blokes who looked to be in their twenties. There was definitely a lack of women in the bar tonight, and the men weren't going to pass up the chance to dance with them.

Beth threw herself into the rhythm of the music, dancing with Jasmine but fully aware of the cute curly redhead who was dancing closer to her. She gave him a smile, and before she knew it she was dancing with him and Jasmine with one of his friends, without a word even being exchanged. She didn't particularly want to exchange words, anyway; the beat of the music filled her ears and her heart, and she let her body move, feeling his arm snake around her waist and their movements synchronise.

She felt a freedom in her movements that the sensible part of her knew was thanks to the copious amounts of wine and multiple shots she had drunk, but gave in to it anyway. Before she knew it, her arms were round his neck, curling into that red hair, and his lips were on hers and then…

No fireworks.

He was cute, he was probably younger than she was, and she could feel beneath her arms that he had a body he worked hard for. And yet the spark… it did not ignite. There was no fire inside her, no desire that made her desperate to be closer, to call a cab and go anywhere to be alone. The kiss broke after a few moments and Beth did not try to re-initiate it. In fact, once the song had ended she made her excuses - although she doubted he could hear her over the noise - and disappeared out into the smoking shelter.

She had no interest in smoking, but the cool breeze and relative quiet gave her a chance to regain control of her swirling, drunken mind. She sat on a step, ignoring the other patrons, and let her head hang forwards.

"Are you okay?" a voice that she did not recognise asked, and when she found the energy to raise her head, she saw it was the red-head from the dance floor. She tried not to let her face show her disappointment in the fact that he had followed her... it wasn't his fault, after all.

"Yeah. Bit warm," she said.

He sat down on the step next to her, leaving her some space which she was grateful for. In the harsh outdoor lighting, she realised he looked a lot younger.

"Sorry," he said. "If it was something I did."

She smiled then, and patted his arm clumsily. "Nothing you did. Honest." She squinted at his slightly blurry face. "How old are you, anyway?" She could have argued that the alcohol was making her bolder, but truth be told she was always fairly direct. Always had been - her mother had always said it was her biggest failing, even though she was fairly sure it was that same mother she'd inherited it from.

"Twenty," he said, blushing red, and Beth groaned.

"You're a baby!"

"I'm not!" he said, clearly offended.

"Sorry, sorry, ignore me. I'm a miserable drunk old woman, who just realised she was making out with a-with someone too young for her. Forgive me."

"You're not old," he said, and she smiled at his sweet words. Really, he didn't seem all bad - just way too young for her, and certainly not a firework starter.

"Thank you for saying that," she said.

"So we established you're not old," he said, with a smile, his cheeks fading back to their normal colour. "And I think drunk is probably a fair assessment, so I won't argue with that one. But why are you miserable?"

"I'm not sure you'd understand," she said with a shrug.

"Try me."

"I'm sure you have better things to do with your time...?"

"Tony," he interjected.

"Tony. I'm Beth."

"Nice to meet you," he said, shaking her hand in a formal way that seemed out of place on the floor of a smoking shelter. "And since you clearly have no interest in making out on the dance floor with me - I'm going to try not to take offence at that - it'll do my reputation far more good if they think I'm out here with you, so go on - why are you miserable?"

"You're very confident for a twenty-year-old, aren't you?"

"Yes," he said with a grin. "And I'm also drunk. Who knows which is more true. And I probably won't even re-member this in the morning, so you might as well tell me."

She looked him up and down for a moment, this blurry figure, this cute, young, interesting *boy*, and thought - *what the hell?* "My life's going nowhere," she said. "I'm stuck. Stuck in a dead-end job, rented flat, no love life to speak of… There's nothing that excites me. I feel like my life is over before I've even hit thirty."

"Told you you weren't old," he said with a crooked smile.

"Go on then, fix all my problems," she said with a daring look.

"Hey, what do I know, I'm just a student on a night out. But I think the answer's pretty obvious…"

"It is?"

"If you're stuck, change something. Move. Get a new job. I would say a new man, but you've turned me down so you're obviously not on the market right now…"

"Cocky as well as cheeky!" she said, but she liked his attitude.

"Seriously, though. You're too young to feel like you should be in a nursing home already. Find a hobby, or charity work, or a new group of friends - changing one thing might make the world of difference. Or, throw caution to the wind and change everything…"

"Are you my guardian angel?" Beth asked, with a hint of sarcasm dripping through her lips.

"Too good looking for that," he said.

It was at that moment that Jasmine appeared in the doorway.

"There you are! I thought you'd gone home with someone."

"She was about to," Tony said, and Beth elbowed him in the ribs.

"No, she wasn't. But I am going to go home. You coming?" She glared at Tony, daring him to answer.

He laughed but stayed silent, and Jasmine nodded, eying the young man suspiciously. "Come on then," she said, offering Beth a hand and helping her to her feet. She wouldn't like to admit it, but she needed the help up - things were swaying a lot more than they should have been.

"Thanks guardian angel," she said, sticking her tongue out at him and laughing as she exited the door. "Sorry for the crappy kiss!"

CHAPTER THREE

"Oh I do like to be beside the seaside…" Beth sang to herself, packing her belongings on the morning of her visit to Devon. Change may have been on her mind, but being organised enough to pack before the day wasn't something that was going to happen anytime soon. The weather looked to be nice, and so she threw in a hodge podge of dresses, shorts and cardis, hoping there would be enough to last her the week. She could generally get away with stealing her sister Lee's clothes in a pinch, although trousers were definitely a no-go - the difference in their heights made that simply comical.

The drive was peaceful, since she had chosen to go in the middle of the day and before any of the school holidays started, and she enjoyed the thrill of speeding down the motorway, the windows slightly open and the music blaring. It became windier as she headed away from the city, merging onto the A road that had twists and turns and a few sheer drops. It was a journey she knew she should make more often - after all, it was only an hour or so.

The sun dazzled across the hot tarmac, and Beth felt a buzz of joy as she sped away from everything that was getting her down at home. She sang badly to whatever came on the radio, and only got lost twice trying to find the winding driveway up to the little cottage that Lee shared with her fiancé James.

It really was a Christmas-card cottage, Beth thought as she parked - although not now, of course, in the sunlight. But you could imagine it covered in snow, with a robin on the fence and Christmas lights in the windows, at Christmas time. It was an old, red brick building, with a white picket fence and herbs growing in the front garden. The windows had shutters although they were all open, and ivy grew up one of the walls.

"Beth!" Lee shouted from an upstairs window, and Beth shaded her eyes to see her sister bathed in sunlight. "Come in, the front door's open, I'm just changing Holly, be down in five."

She dragged her poorly-packed suitcase out of the car and through the front door, taking her shoes off before walking in to the wooden-floored living room. It was all very tidy, she thought, even with a young baby in the house. There were a few toys dotted around, and a half-drunk mug of tea on the coffee table, but other than that everything was in its place. There was a sense of peace around that Beth knew would be broken as soon as her little niece was let loose, and she allowed herself to wallow in it for a few minutes before wandering to check out the photos on the mantelpiece. Some were clearly new; a candid shot of Lee, holding baby Holly at what looked like a few days old; and a family shot of the three of them, James with Holly in a sling, the two adults grinning like fools in front of the crashing waves at the seaside.

A wail announced her sister's entrance, and Beth

turned round to see tall, blonde Lee wearing a black maxi dress, hair thrown up in a bun and a confused looking Holly on her hip.

They hugged, and Beth held her hands out for a baby cuddle.

"Come to Aunty Beth!"

"I've been referring to you as Aunty Elizabeth…" Lee said with a smirk, causing her little sister to smack her on the arm. "Hey! You deserve it, you called me Shirley last week."

"Thank you mother for old fashioned names, eh," Beth said with a grin, jiggling a slightly unsure Holly up and down on her hip to settle her. "Mummy's being mean to me," she confided in the little girl in a loud whisper. "But at least she gave you a sensible name, that you won't need to shorten."

Lee flopped onto the sofa. "Who knows, maybe she'll hate it!"

"James at work?"

"Yeah, he'll be back in time for dinner."

"No work for you today?"

"Nope, taken most of the week off to spend with you, little sister! You sounded like things are a bit rubbish…"

"Let's not talk about that right now…" Beth said with a shrug, passing a now tearful Holly back. "This little lady wants her mummy, not me I'm afraid!"

"It's just because she hasn't seen you in a while," Lee

said, taking back the baby who immediately settled in her arms. "She'll be fine once you've been here a couple of days."

"Let's hope so! Anyway, that conversation can only happen over wine, I'm afraid, so let's wait until a bottle is cracked open before I moan to you about my life."

"Deal. So, what shall we do while you're down? I presume you want to go to the seaside?"

"Definitely. And Dartmouth, always."

"Fish and chips by the water - always good when you're in Devon!"

Beth stretched out on the sofa. "It feels good to get away from everything," she said. "This house feels like it's so far away from everything else in the world."

"I thought it'd be too isolating for someone like you!"

"There was a time when it would have been too isolating for you!" Beth threw back, and Lee nodded.

"Times change, I guess," she said. "It's worked out pretty well for me, I have to say." And Beth had to admit that her sister had never looked so happy than in that moment, sat on the sofa with her daughter, with messy hair and a patch of what looked suspiciously like baby sick on her sleeve.

James was definitely the cook of the family, but Lee and Beth did their best to throw something together so he could come back to a homemade meal. Vegetables were cooked, chicken was grilled and potatoes boiled - handily all while Holly napped. Lee poured a generous glass of wine for Beth, and a much smaller one for herself - "On account of the breast-feeding," she explained.

"You give up a lot when you have a kid, don't you!" Beth said with a large sip of wine.

"It's not so bad. You get a lot too!"

The food was almost ready and Holly had been awake for ten minutes or so when the front door clicked open, and James walked through the door in his uniform, hat in hand. He smiled as soon as he saw them, leaning in kiss Lee and take Holly, swirling in the air as she giggled.

"Hiya Beth," he said. "Lovely to see you!"

"Thanks for having me!" she replied. She realised she'd been wrong earlier - now her sister looked happier than she'd ever seen her. The changes she had made to her life were clearly working - giving stuff up didn't look like much of a hardship when you were that happy.

"You know you're always welcome," he said, running a hand through his dark, curly hair. "I should change - is that dinner I can smell?"

"Almost ready!" Lee answered.

"You should come more often, Beth," he said, with a grin and a twinkle in his eye as he walked up the stairs. Beth watched Lee's eyes follow him.

"You can go after him, if you want," she said with a giggle. "I'm no prude! I can babysit…"

"Elizabeth Davis," she said with a roll of her eyes. "Get

your mind out of the gutter. And I'll remind you that there is a bottle of wine open, and I expect to hear all the gossip on your love life!"

Dinner was a pleasant affair, and James talked about his day (which had been boring, apparently, and involved trying to herd some cows who were blocking a main road. Luckily, none were hurt), and Lee described Holly's attempts at crawling in great detail. A candle was lit in the middle of the table, although it definitely wasn't dark outside yet, and Holly made a mess of the vegetables and chicken she had been given, much to the amusement of the adults present.

Beth sipped her wine quietly while they talked, realising she was quickly becoming in danger of viewing this as some sort of idyll; something she needed to aspire to. As happy and content as they were, she gave herself a mental shake; she didn't need - or even necessarily want - marriage and a baby right now. A carbon copy of her sister's life was not going to solve her lack of enthusiasm for life right now.

"So, how are plans for your wedding going?" she asked, and James offered to wash up as Lee shared photos on her phone of the dresses she was considering for the bridesmaids, of which Beth was to be one.

"Since it's a Christmas wedding," she said, "I thought red. Do you like it?"

Beth nodded. "It doesn't really matter what I think though, sis - it's up to you!"

"I know, but I want you and Gina and James' sisters - well, sister and sisters-in-law - to like what you're wearing."

"You've got your dress, though?"

"Yeah," Lee said with a grin. "I've chosen it, but it needs altering - after all, I'd just had a baby when we got engaged, so my body's changed a bit since then!"

"And you're still not letting any of us see?"

"Nope!" she said, laughing and refilling Beth's wine glass.

"You're trying to get me drunk so I'll spill the beans," Beth said, narrowing her eyes suspiciously.

"Me? Never! Anyway, who knows if there are beans to spill?"

"Between you and mum, you always find out everything..."

"But I don't judge like mum does!" Lee said with a raise of her eyebrows.

"I don't think anyone ever does..."

CHAPTER FOUR

It was in the picturesque town of Dartmouth the next day that it happened.

James was working a later shift, and so the four of them set out for a morning together, with Beth continually surprised by how much *stuff* was required when taking a baby out for the day. The sky was an azure blue and seagulls dotted the skyline when they eventually made it to the water front and took a seat on a thankfully empty wooden bench. The water lapped lazily against the stone wall, with little boats and dinghies bobbing up and down peacefully. A lone gentleman in a blue cap was tending to his boat; a few people milled around opening up shops or snapping photographs, but on the whole the area was still quite quiet. It was only nine in the morning, after all; plenty of time for the area to get busy.

James and Lee chatted, but Beth just soaked in the atmosphere. Across the water, rows of brightly coloured houses stood overlooking the scene, and it was so perfect it almost looked like a painting. A little boat began to move through the water, connecting the two sides of the idyll, creating white foam and waves as it bobbed towards them. Beth let out a sigh without even realising.

"You okay?" Lee asked.

"Yeah... it's just so perfect, isn't it."

"I've always loved it here," Lee agreed. "Since we came down as kids with mum, remember?"

Beth nodded. "But it just seems to get better every time."

James and Lee caught each other's eyes, and let the quiet wash over them all for a moment or two, before Holly's fussing and James' rumbling stomach demanded action.

"Shall we go and get breakfast?" James asked, pointing over at a small café that had opened its doors onto the sunny street. "They're open, and we can have a wander around later."

Beth tore her eyes off the picturesque view and nodded, finding it a struggle to move from the peace of the moment.

"What's over there, then?" she asked, pointing vaguely over at the bright houses as she wolfed down her egg and sausage sandwich.

"That's Kingswear," James said, happy to use his local knowledge. "There's not much over there, other than what you can see - although, Agatha Christie - you know, the mystery writer? - she lived over there, towards Galmpton, so there's her house which you can visit. Apparently she got a lot of inspiration for her books from there, and set some around here."

"Yeah, one of the Poirot episodes was filmed on Burgh Island, wasn't it?" Lee chimed it, grabbing a bit of her own food while Holly was occupied with some toast.

"Yeah, that's right. And one at Greenway, I think. I've never read any of them, I have to admit," James said. "Watched a few with mum and dad though."

"Never read any Agatha Christie?" Beth said with a gasp of mock outrage. "Lee and I devoured them when we were younger."

"Those copies at mum's are so well read," Lee agreed. "It's been years though, since I last read one..."

They wandered the picturesque little shops together, picking up a cute new outfit for Holly - yellow, with sunshines and daisies embroidered on it - and spending too long for Holly's liking in a boutique little jewellery store that had one-off pieces designed around crystals and birth stones. They ummed and ahhed over several pieces, but ended up leaving with nothing in the end - although both debated their wisdom in doing so all the way down the street, and almost turned back.

They found themselves in a second hand bookshop down a small alleyway near lunch time, with a strict time limit due to James' need to get back for work in the afternoon.

"Look, Lee!" Beth called out from a dusty corner near the back of the narrow shop. "Loads of Agatha Christies! If there was ever a time to reread..." She browsed the titles, moving her finger across the dusty spines as she read. *And then there were none; Murder on the Orient Express; The Mousetrap...* All ones she had read, as Lee commented over her shoulder, but the pull of rereading them was strong, and she left the shop with three in a paper bag, as well as a leather-bound notebook she hadn't been able to resist. Well, she reasoned with herself, she was on holiday, after all - and it was a very cheap holiday, all things considered.

"We'd better head back, I'm afraid," James said, checking his watch as he bounced the baby on his hip.

"I did promise I'd meet someone at two," Lee said apologetically. "About some possible legal issues they're having. I won't be too long, I promise."

"It's fine," Beth said breezily, as they wandered back past the boats bobbing on the water. "Although, actually... would it be rude if I stayed here? Unless you need me to take care of Holly or anything..."

"No, no, I was just going to take her with me anyway... If you're sure? We can pick you up later if you like."

"Or I can get a bus, don't worry about me! I just feel like I wouldn't mind spending a bit longer out here, if that's okay."

"It's your holiday," Lee said, giving her a hug. "I want you to have a good time. Relax, enjoy the sunshine, ring me for a lift, okay?"

"Will do. See you later!"

She waved them off and sat back on the bench, closing her eyes and hearing the gulls, the people, the water...

The sun felt glorious on her skin, and she took a deep breath and felt free as her lungs filled with the slightly salty air. She could definitely smell fish and chips in the distance, and thought that might not be a bad idea for her lunch... but for now, she cracked open one of the books she had bought, crossed her legs on that wooden bench and let herself get lost in the mysterious world of Agatha Christie.

She was halfway through the novel when it happened. When she decided what the change in her life was going to be. It wasn't a small one, by any means - but then hadn't Tony said change was good? Change was what she needed? She wasn't sure why she was listening so much to the words of a rambling drunk twenty-year-old... except that the words had certainly resonated with her. It was what she had known she needed to do - she just needed someone to tell her. And now she knew what that change should be.

CHAPTER FIVE

She would move to Dartmouth.

It sounded simple, as she said it there in her head, over and over. She would move to Dartmouth. She felt happy here. It was beautiful here. Her soul felt like it soared here.

Well, she certainly felt poetic here, that was for sure.

She let out a breath and laughed, causing a couple of passers-by to look on in confusion and concern, as the petite blonde sat and laughed to herself, alone on a bench.

Of course, there would be organisation needed - something she wasn't great at. But her sister had done it, and things had worked out well for her - and as much as she knew she didn't want a carbon copy of her sister's life, this just felt right. She could be near family, for a start. She could find some new job - after all, it was a tourist town with summer right around the corner, there was bound to be some work, right?

She could start again. Hit refresh and see if things worked better this time around...

The idea seemed a lot crazier as the day went on. Her

mind was too jumpy after the thought hit her to carry on reading, so she stashed the book back in its paper bag and hit the shops again. She found herself back in that same little jewellery store, where the owner gave a wide grin.

"I thought you'd be back!"

"Couldn't resist," said Beth, touching the delicate chains with the tip of her finger. She knew Lee had loved the silver bracelet, with intricate silver strands entwined around tiny nuggets of turquoise. It was the golden tiger's eye necklace that had caught Beth's eye - a large piece of golden brown crystal attached to a fine gold chain that caught the sunlight. They were both a little more than Beth should really have been spending on jewellery, but they had been on her mind all day, and she knew if she went home without them she'd regret it.

Just then, her phone buzzed in her pocket and she couldn't help but smile when she read the words on the screen.

If you have time, could you go back and buy that bracelet Lee liked? I'll give you the money this evening! Thanks - James.

She took a quick selfie in front of the jewellery counter and sent it back, with the caption *Great minds think alike!* Her decision made, she went to the counter and watched as the woman carefully wrapped them in tissue paper, before placing them into a midnight blue bag covered in moons and stars.

He was definitely a good man, she thought as she walked out of the shop and headed to the fish and chip shop, her stomach rumbling despite the decent sized breakfast she'd eaten that morning. Beth had never been overly keen on Nathan, Lee's cheating ex - there'd always seemed something a little slimy about him, although she'd never voiced this. They'd appeared happy together, for a long time, and so Beth had been polite and friendly to her brother-in-law. If she ever saw him again, though... he'd be sorry.

She tried to think back to whether Lee had ever seemed this happy, this relaxed, when she was with Nathan, and thought that she couldn't have been... this was a very different Lee. The old Lee was extremely concerned with things following a plan, and was always out working or exhausted from work. She certainly didn't have leisurely breakfasts or cook dinner and laugh over it.

I'm going to move to Dartmouth.

It was definitely a crazy idea - but then she had once been known for her crazy ideas. And maybe crazy was what she needed right now.

There was a short queue at the fish and chip shop, which boasted that everything was cooked fresh to order, and Beth watched a younger guy in surfer shorts balance three boxes of food as he left, then a family argue over how many portions of chips they needed. She ordered and then perused the notices on the board in the window as she waited.

Missing dog - reward for safe return. Jack Russell, ginger tipped tail. Call 07391 283103

Garage sale! Everything must go! From 12pm on July 1st. 5 Church Street - great bargains!

1 bedroom flat. £500/month, bills included, access through chip shop. References required. Sorry, not suitable for pets.

It hit her like a force, like kismet, like some God or fate was giving her a sign. A big, glowing arrow that said 'this is what you need to do!'

"This flat," she said to the young guy who was packaging up her fish and chips. "Is it above this shop?"

He nodded and pointed to a white door to his right. "Yep, right through there. The owner used to live up there, but he's got married and moved."

"Is it still available?"

"As far as I know - think it's empty from July 1st."

"Can you see the water from it?"

"Give me ten minutes and I can show you around, if you like? My colleague will come back from lunch then."

She nodded and smiled. "Sounds great. I'll eat this outside then come back, okay?"

As she tucked in to her traditional Devon fare, she felt as though perhaps things were slotting into place.

"Bedroom," he said, pointing to a small white room with a double bed taking up the majority of the space.

"Is the furniture going?" Beth asked.

"No, I think it's being rented as furnished, although the

bedding will be gone, and there's still clothes in the wardrobe I think. Then that's the kitchen..." A small kitchen opened out onto a living room with a two seater sofa, television and coffee table - but Beth barely noticed them. It was the view that got her - from the living room window, you could see the bobbing boats and the tiny little multicoloured houses, as well as the water and the people walking below.

"Perfect," she said. "What a view. How is this not rented yet?"

He shrugged. "Some people don't like living above a chip shop, apparently! Plus it's only one bedroom, lots of families or couples looking right now."

"I love it," she said. "I want it."

She hadn't been impulsive in a long time; it was a lot of money, and she was still renting in Exeter... she had no job, she had no plan, nothing except a longing to live in this town and read mystery novels and see that view every single day...

"Great! I'll give you the owner's number, and you can talk it through with him, is that okay? He's gonna be so pleased someone wants it! He loves this place."

CHAPTER SIX

She contemplated her decision as she rode the bus back to Totnes, ignoring Lee's kind offer of a lift. She needed the time to figure out what she was going to say to her sensible older sister who, despite making that leap herself, might not be so impressed at her little sister doing the same.

She'd called the owner - a Mr Tim Hutchins - as soon as she'd left the flat, and pending references from her current landlord, he was thrilled to have her move in.

"Can you move in from the first?" he'd asked, and without thinking she'd agreed, knowing there'd be details to sort down the line.

"Well, I'll wait for the reference - you said you'd contact the landlord?"

"Yeah," Beth said, thinking she'd better give notice herself before asking for a reference.

"And then if all looks good we can sign a contract by the end of the week!"

"What do you mean, you're moving to Dartmouth?"

Lee asked as the three of them ate dinner that evening.

"I'm done with Exeter, sick of my job," she admitted, spooning mashed potato into Holly's mouth as Lee sat with her mouth open at Beth's news. "I love Dartmouth. I can be closer to you..."

"What will you do for work?"

"Figure it out!" she said with a forced laugh, "Like I've always done!"

"But Beth... you can't just decide on a whim to move your whole life to Devon because you like the place."

Beth was a little insulted by this. "You did."

It was said a little more harshly than she perhaps meant to, and the words stung.

"Okay, yes, I did, but my life had already been ripped to shreds when I made that decision. I caught my husband in the middle of having an affair, if you'd forgotten." It was the closest the two had come to an argument in many years - possibly since they were still teenagers, living at home together.

"But you still left everything else - house, job, friends. My life is empty, Lee, so I'm ripping it to shreds myself. I want to do this."

"Beth - just because it worked for me doesn't mean it necessarily will for you," she said, biting her lip. "I don't want you to throw your whole life away because I did."

"I'm my own person, Lee. I can make this decision for myself. It's not that I want your life - I just want a different life."

"In Dartmouth?"

"In Dartmouth. I've fallen in love with the place, more than I have with a man in a long time. And I've found somewhere to live…"

"What? How long has this been the plan?"

Beth glanced at her watched. "About six hours," she said with a slight grin.

Lee ran a hand through her hair.

"You exhaust me," she said with a sigh.

"Says the woman who moved to a new town, found a flat mate and set up a business, all while supposedly still planning to head back home?"

"Fair point," Lee said after a moment's silence. "It'll be lovely having you so close… I'm sorry Beth, I don't want to be all… *mum* on you. It just stresses me out."

"It'll be fine," she said, more confident than she truly felt. "It'll all slot into place, I'm sure of it."

They clinked glasses, Beth's full of wine, Lee's apple juice, and toasted. "To Dartmouth then," Lee said.

"To Dartmouth," Beth answered, ignoring the knot of worry in her stomach at what she had decided to do.

Maybe she needed Lee's help; she was the organised one. She had always been very good at writing lists, as Beth recalled…

Lee and James had clearly talked that evening once Beth was in bed, as the next day he knew about Beth's plans, although he didn't pass any judgment on them. Lee and James were both off, and so a plan had been made to head to the beach in Thurlestone, a little village twenty minutes away, with the hope of braving a swim in the sea and some paddling for Holly.

Beth had woken excited, even if it was tinged with nerves, and realised she couldn't remember the last time she had got up feeling a sense of purpose. It was good, she decided - and the landlord hadn't seemed too miffed at her giving notice over the phone the night before, so she hoped that her reference would be good. That would be one thing ticked off the list, at least.

James drove, and Beth sat in the front, with Lee in the back keeping Holly happy. Beth was quite happy to be driven, especially on roads this winding with such high hedges, and when she saw the amount of times James had to reverse for oncoming traffic, she was pleased she hadn't offered. It was all worth it, though, when they turned a corner and saw the glittering sea nestled between cliffs and fields at the bottom of the valley.

"Wow," said Beth.

"Takes my breath every time," Lee agreed, craning her neck slightly to see between the front seats. "With the sun reflecting off it like that..."

There were a few cars parked in the car park, but it wasn't too busy yet, despite the ever-increasing heat. Together they bundled Holly and everything they had brought with them - food, towels, shade, suncream - out of the car and to a patch of golden sand that they decided to claim. James busied himself setting up enough shade for Holly, while Lee focussed on covering their daughter with suncream.

Beth scrunched her feet into the sand, feeling the grains between her toes and tickling the soles of her feet. Her shoes had come off the second they'd left concrete, and the sparkling sea ahead called out to her.

"Anyone else going to be up for swimming?" she asked, stripping down to her bikini in preparation.

"It'll be far too cold for Holly," Lee said. "And probably for me too! I'm happy paddling."

"Spoil sport," Beth said, sticking her tongue out. "James?"

"Definitely up for swimming," he said, looking pleased with the shaded area he'd set up. He was already wearing his swimming trunks, and stripped off his t-shirt in a single movement, showing off - whether intentionally or not - his impressive physique. He had the muscles of someone who clearly kept in shape, and Beth couldn't help an appreciative look, before averting her gaze and realising that her sister's eyes were most definitely fixated on her fiancé.

"Come and paddle then Lee, while we swim."

"Do you not want to get warm first?" Lee asked, pulling off her own beach dress and adding it to the heap on the floor, a little less confidently than Beth or James. After the birth of her first child, she couldn't help but feel a little self-conscious of her changed body; Beth planned to privately tell her she had nothing to worry about. She still looked fantastic, as she always had done.

"Race you down there!" Beth said, setting off down the beach at a slow run, feeling the warm air swirling around her. She glanced back behind her and saw she was in no danger of losing; James was not in pursuit. No, he only had eyes for his fiancée, and the two seemed to sharing a moment than Beth felt like an intruder observing - but she struggled to look away. The tender way they kissed...

She moved away, dipping her toes in the water and wincing a little at how cold it actually was. The warm weather belied the temperature of the sea before them.

"It'll be fine once you're in, honest," James said, having jogged to catch up with her. "Getting in's the worst part!"

He took a deep breath and slid into the water, releasing a gasp of air as the coldness hit him, then moving his arms through the sea in a powerful breast stroke.

"See? Lovely now!"

"Hmmm," Beth responded in disbelief, but took a deep breath and plunged herself - with far less grace - into the water. She shrieked a little, but found he was right: the sharp iciness wore off once you were in, and it was insanely refreshing.

Lee had caught up to them with Holly, who had crawled part of the way and been carried the rest when she tried to put a handful of sand in her mouth.

Beth copied James for a few minutes, cutting through the water in laps with a passable breast stroke, and enjoying the feeling of the water surrounding her body, making her feel weightless. She lay back in water, feeling the chill engulf her hair and her scalp, floating on her back and squinting up at the bright sky above. She knew this was not an everyday moment, lying in the sea and staring up at a cloudless sky, but it felt pretty beautiful.

She stood - the water was fairly shallow, even once she'd swum out a little - and shielded her eyes against the sunlight to watch Holly jumping tiny waves, with Lee lifting her by the arms every time one approached. She was giggling away, clearly not put off by the cold temperatures.

"I love it here!" Beth shouted, and Lee grinned.

"If you're moving here, that's definitely a positive!"

"I don't know how you're not at the beach every day," she said into the warm breeze, lying back again to float on the salty water.

"Life!" Lee replied, and Beth knew she had a point...

But this bliss was something she wouldn't forget for a while.

CHAPTER SEVEN

Life moved very quickly after that week. Gone were the monotonous tasks that never seemed to change. Instead, Beth attempted to achieve the tasks on the list she had sat and written with Lee on her last night, over wine and complaints about what her current life had become.

Hand in notice.
Pack.
Send first month's rent.
Find a job.
Sort out utilities.
Hire a van.

She was sure much more would come up as the next two weeks flew by, but it was a good starting point. She'd started with the notice, and while they'd said they were sad to see her go, they were happy to take two weeks notice plus the remainder of her holiday in lieu of the rest of the time she owed, and so she was good to go for July 1st. Her flat would have to be paid for two weeks after leaving, but there was no getting out of that - such was life, she thought, chalking it up to the costs of spontaneity.

The one person who was not so impressed was Jasmine, when she broke the news at their first lunch together on the Monday after her week away.

"You were meant to be going on holiday for a week, Beth," she said, "Not abandoning me forever!"

"Dramatic as ever!" Beth said with a laugh as they drank iced coffees and shared a large slice of chocolate cake.

"Seriously, though - you're upping and leaving?"

"Yep, seems that way!"

As with everyone else she'd told, the plan was received with a mixture of shock and disbelief.

"Just seems very out of the blue..."

"As you said, I'm not that old yet! If I can't be spontaneous now, when can I be? Besides, I decided that change is what I need..."

"Please do not tell me you are making life-changing decisions based on a drunken conversation with an inebriated teenager that you made out with for all of five minutes?"

Beth gave her a gentle shove. "No I am not. And he wasn't a teenager... and he was quite cute, if I remember correctly, there were just-"

"No fireworks. I get the drill. I presume you think there'll be fireworks in Dartmouth? Or is there someone there already?" Beth laughed at the way her eyes lit up at the possibility of some gossip.

"No there isn't, and I've decided I'm done firework-chasing. I'm going because I love the place and I need to decide what I want in my life - and a man will not solve that for me."

"Very modern," Jasmine said, licking the last of the chocolate from her spoon. "But when there is a man, you won't forget all about me with the gossip, will you?"

"*If* there is a man at any point, I promise I will give you all the details."

"I'll miss you," Jasmine said, for once without any hint of drama or irony.

"Me too," Beth said, reaching over and squeezing her hand. "But I need to do this. And before you know it, you'll be moving on somewhere else too - or marrying IT guys…"

The documents had all been signed for the flat before she'd even left Lee's the previous week, when she'd briefly met her new landlord, Tim. She thought he was probably in his late thirties, slightly overweight with a black beard and a penchant for wearing Hawaiian shirts - but he seemed like a pleasant enough guy, and was thrilled when Beth enthused over the views from the flat as much as he did.

Paying the first month's rent was a simple task of logging on to her account and putting in his details - although she was slightly stressed to find the amount pretty much wiped out her savings. It made the 'get a job' point on her list far more imperative - but she found trying to find a job whilst not actually living there to be difficult. Besides, the whole point was to find things she loved - and nothing was sparking her joy at that moment in time as she perused the vacancies on job-search websites.

Packing was a chore that she had always hated. It was one of the reasons she had become a little less spontaneous when it came to her living arrangements - she dreaded the packing. She had too much stuff, which she knew, and as she surveyed it all at the end of the working week she groaned.

"Where on earth do I even start?" she said to herself. She'd managed to nab a load of boxes that were about to be crushed at work, and so started with the the living room first. Thankfully the place was furnished, so it was only her own personal affects she needed to worry about - but boy there were a lot of them. She began shoving throws and cushions into a box, then tipped them all out again and began to fold them when she realised how quickly she was running out of space. Clothes, shoes and handbags were definitely the next hurdle to tackle, and try as she might to be brutal about throwing things away, she still found herself with the majority of the items that had been in her wardrobe now stacked inside boxes by her front door. She tried very hard to think what Lee would do, and eventually labelled the boxes with the room they were for, feeling like that counted as some organisation at least.

Feeling exhausted, she poured herself an exceptionally large glass of wine, put the television on and decided enough was enough for one evening. She still had a week left - she was sure she would get it all done.

Famous. Last. Words.

The day of her big move arrived, and Beth realised

not only had she not packed up any of the kitchen, but she had also completely forgotten the last item on her list: hire a van. She surveyed the mountain of boxes that would most definitely not fit in her tiny car and swore repeatedly, wondering who she could phone for help. Lee? She would be busy with Holly. Her mother? She hadn't exactly told her mother she was moving yet… she was planning on following Lee's tried and tested approach of moving first and telling their mother later.

Jasmine was the only name she could come up with that she wasn't embarrassed to admit this failing to, and when she got through on the fourth ring, she was pleased that she had made the call.

"Not that I want to help you abscond from Exeter," she said with a huff, "But Joe has a van, and I'm sure I can persuade him to give you a hand."

"Really? You'd be a lifesaver. With a car and a van, I think we should manage it!"

"No problem. Let me talk to him, we'll be at yours in an hour or so, 'kay?"

"I'll be ready - or try to be at least!"

It was just under an hour later when a knock on to door made Beth jump up from her frenzied last-minute packing and realise that it was time to get moving. Jasmine bounced through the door, pulling Joe along behind her. Beth had met him once or twice, and she thanked him profusely as he began lugging boxes down the stairs to his van.

"Thanks for coming too," Beth said as she and Jasmine took a box each and stepped carefully down the narrow stairs.

"I get to be nosy and see where you're moving to - it's a win for me!"

"Let's just hope we can fit it all in," Beth said.

It felt like an endless trudge up and down the stairs with box after box, but eventually both the van and Beth's little Fiat were full to the brim, and the flat was mercifully empty of boxes.

"I just need to check a couple of things," Beth said, handing them a piece of paper with the address on. "And probably get fuel. See you there?"

As she wandered her now empty flat, she marvelled at how much bigger it was without all of her stuff inside. Even with the furniture remaining, it felt much more spacious - and she wondered whether someone else was waiting for their own fresh start which they would get in this flat. She said goodbye in her head, feeling a little silly - especially as it was technically hers for two more weeks - and locked the door behind her.

"Time to go."

The journey seemed quicker this time round, and Beth found herself anticipating the feeling of walking into that flat again, seeing that view. The fact that the money for petrol, and the money she knew she needed to offer Jasmine and Joe for their fuel, was pretty much the end of her overdraft was something she tried very hard to push to the back of her mind. It would work out - she needed to believe that. Lee and James had invited her over for dinner the following evening, so that was at least one night's food sorted. And the deposit from her current flat would help her back into the black - she just needed to wait for it all to come through.

It'll work out, she told herself, picturing the boats on the water and the ice cream van by the side of the road.

After stopping for fuel - as expected, she was pretty much on empty - she arrived a little while after Jasmine and her boyfriend, but she grinned as she caught sight of them sat on the wall by the water, enjoying an ice-cream in the June sunshine.

"I guess I can see the attraction," Jasmine said, hopping off from the wall without messing up her clothes, and walking over to where Beth stood waiting.

"Right? It's pretty spectacular, isn't it."

"I mean, I'm not sure it'd make me up and move my whole life..." she said with a roll of her eyes, but Beth just rolled hers straight back. "But yes, it is spectacular. Glad we found the right place - some of those roads are bit of a nightmare, aren't they!"

"Don't I know it. That's one thing I'm not looking forward to - learning how to reverse down a narrow road!"

"Rather you than me."

Beth greeted the young guy that was running the chip shop that day, and used her new set of keys to open up the door to the flat. Together, they shifted the boxes upstairs - a task which took far longer than packing them into the van, it seemed - and dumped them into an intimidating pyramid in the centre of the room. Beth's eye caught the glinting light from the water outside her window, and she felt calmer about the hours of unpacking ahead of her. It was okay; this would be fine. She had no deadline. She wanted change - well, this was certainly change.

"Ring me, soon, okay?" Jasmine said as they said goodbye for the third time. Joe tapped his fingers on the steering wheel, clearly forcing a smile to remain on his face.

"You can ring me too, you know!"

"Yeah, yeah, but you know how rubbish I am."

Beth laughed. "I'll ring, I promise. Thank you, for today - and please give Joe that petrol money. Thanks Joe!" she shouted, hoping he could hear her through the closed doors. He raised a hand in farewell, then started the engine - a clear sign that the time for goodbyes was over.

Beth watched the van drive away until it was a dot, and then it was gone, round a corner and on its journey back to Exeter.

It was just her now. Her, Dartmouth, and a little flat above a chip shop.

Well, things had definitely changed...

CHAPTER EIGHT

When she awoke the next morning, it took her several minutes to remember where on earth she was. The bed, the bedding, the ceiling, the light streaming through the windows - all of it felt very different. As did the fact that it was a week day and, aside from unpacking, she had no commitments. Nowhere to be, no-one expecting her - not until dinner that evening at James and Lee's.

She decided she had time for the luxury of another half an hour in bed. She'd left the curtains open so she could still see that beautiful vista, and rolled over to face the sunshine over the water as she stretched her aching limbs. As moves went, yesterday had been fairly simple, but there still seemed to be that slight sense of trauma that came with making a massive change to anything in life.

There were many worries on her mind, but she pushed them successfully into a corner for now. There was time for that later - plenty of time. For now, she had a comfortable bed, a beautiful view, and a half-read Agatha Christie to finish.

Bliss.

The day disappeared without Beth really knowing where it had gone. She discovered one roll of toilet roll had been left for her in the bathroom cupboard, and knew she needed either a shop or to 'borrow' from Lee's house that evening. A wander around town, some lunch, a cup of tea watching people wandering up and down, doing their shopping or enjoying the warm air... and then before she knew it, it was time to head over to Totnes, for a promised home-cooked dinner.

She relied heavily on her sat-nav to find the way, nearly missing the turn off to the cottage once again, but she was only five minutes later than she'd said when she eventually turned off the engine and entered the little cottage. There was an amazing smell coming from the kitchen when Lee let her in, and the sisters embraced before heading into the kitchen, where Beth declined a glass of wine since she was driving.

James was standing by the hob, stirring something which had steam swirling up from it with a wooden spoon, with a smiling Holly on his hip.

"Cooking and taking care of the baby?" Beth said with a raised eyebrow. "You know some people would say you're spoilt, Shirley Davis," Beth said, and Lee grinned and for once didn't tell her sister off for using her given name. When they were kids, and they'd annoyed one another, one of their favourite taunts was using each other's full names round the playground for all the other children to hear. It was mortifying - and yet ridiculous, since their full names had of course been read out in the register at some point or another, and they could easily get each other back with the same treatment.

Nowadays, it was more of a joke - although depending on their moods, there may or may not be a laugh.

"He's not completely perfect," Lee said brushing her hand against his arm as she passed him.

"Bet you can't think of ways he's not," Beth answered, holding out her hands for Holly who seemed a little less reticent this time.

"Dinner'll be ready in five," James said, having not responded to the compliments that made him blush a little. "Coq au vin, I hope you're hungry!"

"Starving," she said. "I am unemployed, remember! Sounds very fancy."

"I've had a day off," he said with a shrug. "I like cooking!"

"See? Perfect," Beth stage-whispered to her sister, and they laughed as they sat down at the table in the same seats as when Beth had been staying.

"So, little sister. Dartmouth. How is it?"

"Amazing," Beth said, her eyes lighting up as she spoke. "It feels great being there. I love my flat - you'll have to come over sometime this week, once I've sorted things out a bit."

"And on the job front?"

"Haven't looked yet - that's tomorrow's job."

"Get the local newspapers," James chimed in, handing out the plates of chicken casserole that made Beth's mouth water. "There's usually three or four on sale, covering different areas - and check the notice boards in shops, too. Can't beat local knowledge."

"Thanks, James," Beth said. "Sounds like a good start for tomorrow."

"And you know," Lee said, quietly, although Beth was pretty sure James could still hear her, "You only need to ask. I can always help you out."

Beth put her hand on her sister's arm and gave it a light squeeze. "I know, Lee. I know you've always got my back. But I want to do this on my own. I feel like it's the right decision for me - so hopefully I can make it work."

"You always make things work," Lee said with a grin, tucking in. "Ever since we were kids you made impossible situations work out for you."

"So did you!"

"But mine was sheer hard work. Yours was something else... personality, maybe!"

Beth grinned. "Well, with a record like that, things have got to work out, haven't they!"

Feeling happily full after the home-cooked meal James had served, Beth returned home feeling calm. The suggestions of places to job-hunt would be a good project for the days to come, and she felt confident there must be something she could do that would earn her some money. For now, however, adrenaline seemed to course through her veins, the excitement of being in a new place, of seeing the moon reflecting in the water, broken only by the occasional ripple from a duck or bird, made her want to explore. As she stared over to Kingswear and saw the full moon hanging bright, illuminating the houses but distorting their happy, bright colours into something a little more foreboding, she could see how mysteries could be inspired by this place.

The sea, she decided - that was what she wanted. A quick search online found the nearest beach, and within five minutes she was in the car, traversing the unknown roads and following the directions from the voice inside the phone. Excitement bubbled within her, feeling like she was breaking some sort of rule, sneaking out at night - she'd always loved the feeling of rebelling, even if she'd never done anything *that* audacious. Well, audacious by her mother's standards, but certainly not by her own.

The road curved elegantly around sharp falls, and beyond that - although she tried to not let herself be distracted from the road - Beth could see the sea, dappled in silver moonlight. It wasn't long before she parked up, and rushed to reach the shingle, enjoying the crunching of the pebbles beneath her trainers.

She let out a laugh that hovered in the air around her, taking in deep breaths of the salty air and enjoying the near emptiness of the beach. She thought it must be around ten, although she hadn't bothered to check the time when she'd set out on her adventure. The pebbles turned to sand as Beth approached the water, and the waves crashed half-heartedly onto it. Beth couldn't resist taking her shoes off and dipping her toes in, and was surprised that it wasn't nearly as cold as when she had swum in the sea at Thurlestone with James a couple of weeks previously. Perhaps the two weeks had made that much of a difference; perhaps the sea had heated up significantly through the long, warm summer's day that they'd had; or perhaps it was all relative to the temperature around her. Either way, Beth didn't care; it was a glorious feeling to take off her slightly sweaty shoes and socks and plunge her feet into that oasis.

She glanced around; there didn't seem to be anyone close by, and the lure of that water was too much to deny. Ignoring her mother's many warnings - don't swim in the dark, don't swim alone, don't take your clothes off in public - Beth pulled her dress over her head without much thought and waded into the water wearing nothing but her matching black lace underwear set.

The water embraced her, feeling silken against her skin, and she swam silently through patches of silver, hearing only the rhythmic movement of her own arms and legs in the water. It was a totally different experience to swimming in the day time; she felt free from all constraints. Free from all the expectations she'd been putting on herself, free from the fears that had been pulling her down.

She lay on her back and as the water soaked through her blonde bun, she closed her eyes and let the gentle swish of the waves move her slowly backwards and forwards.

And then she heard a voice.

CHAPTER NINE

"Don't get pulled out, there's no-one around to save you."

She shrieked a little and put her feet down, then ended up with her face partially submerged when she realised that, somehow, she had drifted away from the shore and was now out of her depth. It was only a moment of panic - she was a fairly confident swimmer usually and the current was not strong - but it took her a second to get her breath back and move herself in towards the shore so she could easily stand.

She blinked furiously to get the salt water from her eyes, then looked around frantically for the mysterious male voice. Her heart rate sped up, half in panic, half in curiosity - as she finally spied a man swimming length-distance laps backwards and forwards ahead of her. With his dark hair, she'd almost not spotted him, and she was pleased to know the voice hadn't been in her head. That would have just been too strange to explain...

As her heart rate slowly dipped back to a more normal speed, she watched him moving through the water, slicing through the waves with a powerful front crawl. Even in the low moonlight she could see the muscles in his arms, and the stamina he had for swimming relentlessly, backwards and forwards, seemingly unaware that he was being watched.

But he couldn't be unaware - could he? He'd spoken to her, after all, even if she'd not really acknowledged him. He had probably saved her from her own stupidity, stopped her from drifting out much farther and struggling to get back to shore.

It took a good ten minutes, possibly even fifteen, before he took a break. Beth was still rooted to the spot, although she'd dipped her shoulders under to try to stop herself from visibly shivering. It had been fine while she was moving, but she didn't feel she could swim away, as embarrassed as she was to be caught floating in her underwear dangerously far from the shore - not until she'd spoken to him.

A further minute passed before he seemed to realise she was still there, and when he swam over, Beth found herself struggling to think of what to say.

"Are you all right?" he asked, a slight harshness to his voice that she thought could possibly be from the exertion of all that swimming.

Beth nodded struggling to find words at that moment.

"What are you doing swimming on your own at this time?" Perhaps it wasn't just the exertion - his words still sounded stroppy.

"I could ask you the same thing," Beth said, finding her tongue at last.

He ran a hand through his wet hair and laughed.

"Fair enough. I should say, what are you doing nearly drowning at this time of night?"

"I was not nearly drowning!" Beth replied, incensed.

"You were floating out of your depth without realising, that definitely leads to drowning. And there's no lifeguard here to save you…"

"You could have saved me," she said, and realised to her horror that she was pandering to this man. Just because he was stood there, covered in water droplets, glistening in the moonlight with muscles that made her feel… No. She was not going to humour this man, no matter what his stupid body looked like.

He didn't have an answer for that.

"You scared the living daylights out of me," Beth accused; if he could be stroppy, she could be just as difficult back.

"Sorry."

Their eyes never broke from one another's, and Beth felt a tingling in her arms that could have been from the coolness of the water - or could've been from all her hairs standing on edge.

"Me too," Beth said, holding out her hand. "I'm Beth. Thanks for stopping me floating away."

He eyed her hand suspiciously for a moment or two, before taking it and saying "I'm Cas. And sorry for scaring you."

She found her mind searching for words as the tingle

from where his hand touched hers travelled through her cold body.

"Cas?"

"Short for Caspian," he said with a shrug.

"Caspian..." she let the name roll on her tongue. "I don't think I've ever met a Caspian before."

He folded his arms a little awkwardly. "My mum loves the sea, so..."

"It's a great name."

"Not when you're eight," he said, with a dark look, and Beth laughed, then stopped herself - the look on his face suggested she was being rude.

"Sorry, sorry! It's just my name's Elizabeth, and my sister's is Shirley, and we're always complaining about our old-fashioned names - it's why we always shorten them."

The look on Caspian's face softened a little, and then Beth's teeth chattered embarrassingly of their own accord.

"You should get out. You're going to make yourself ill, stood there not swimming." She nodded, feeling like she couldn't argue with his direct tone - and also knowing that she had been cold for quite a while now.

They swam back to the shore together in silence, Beth enjoying the feeling of blood moving through her limbs once more as she moved through the black expanse. He was faster than her, of course, and she watched him exit the water in his black trunks, water cascading from his dark hair and head to a rock a few metres away from where she had carelessly dumped her dress and trainers. He was already vigorously rubbing his hair with a towel by the time she reached the shore, and she steeled herself to not think about the fact that she was dripping wet in her underwear with no way to dry off, in front of a stranger. After all, underwear was hardly that different from a bikini - and at least it was matching...

She wandered over to her clothes, rubbing her arms in a futile attempt to warm up, and picked up her dress, shoes and socks. There was no other option - she hadn't really thought this plan through when she'd left the house. She'd just have to put the dress back over her wet bra and knickers, dash to the car and blast the heating on, then maybe have a hot shower when she got home.

She was pulling the dress over her head when she felt a much warmer hand on her cold arm, and she jumped - although thankfully didn't shriek this time.

"It's damp, but you can use my towel if you want to," he offered, holding out a black towel that looked like heaven in that moment.

She dropped her dress back onto the shingle and met his gaze for a moment. She appreciated that he kept his eyes on her eyes, and not on the sight she was presenting stood there in just her underwear. She really should have listened to her mother... never strip off in public.

The towel helped extract most of the water from her hair, and while she couldn't dry her underwear, she could at least make sure her skin was dry. At the last moment - and after a quick check to make sure he was behind his rock, she removed her bra and threw her dress on over the top. One fewer piece of wet clothing was surely better.

While she waited to return the towel, not wanting to disturb him as he changed - although, a little voice inside her head admitted she was quite intrigued at that thought - she tried to put her hair back into its bun, but without a hairbrush she was pretty sure she looked like she'd been dragged through a hedge backwards.

He reappeared as silently as he had done in the water, and without words she handed the towel over to him.

"I might not be here to save you next time," he said, a slight smile playing on his lips. "Don't get yourself in trouble again."

"Thanks for the towel, and the near heart attack... Caspian." And then he was gone, walking off on a path that led to an unknown destination, the opposite direction to the car park. She watched him walk, barefoot, shoes and towel in hand, for a few moments, before the night air became too much for her cold skin and she jogged back to her car, feeling grateful for the blast of warm air the heating provided.

It was only when she was on the winding road back to Dartmouth that she realised her bra must have been tangled up in that towel...

CHAPTER TEN

Beth slept better that night than she had done in a long time, and when she awoke to clouds outside her window, she couldn't even be annoyed at the change in weather. She'd had a gloriously hot shower the night before that had washed away the salt, the cold and some of the embarrassment at leaving her bra in the towel of a good-looking stranger. She just hoped he didn't think it was on purpose... that would be even more mortifying.

This morning, though, was not about swimming in the sea, or dark-haired strangers that swam late at night... no, today was for job hunting. She had a list, thoughtfully written by Lee, of course, and she was ready to find what it was that she wanted to do with her life - or at least the next few months of her life, for now.

"Morning Sam," she called to the young guy behind the counter as she headed out of the shop. Sam was busy doing something important-looking with the fryers, and only raised a hand in greeting, but that was plenty for Beth. First stop was the local shop to check out their ad board and buy the local newspapers. Perusing the board, she decided there was nothing of too much interest on it - except for an advert for a local boat tour, which she thought might be good once she had a little more disposable income - but she bought three local newspapers, and took them to her favourite bench over-looking the moody water.

As she approached, she felt her heart sink slightly as she noticed a white-haired gentleman in an oversized, green overcoat sat there, enjoying what she thought was a bacon butty - but she powered on and sat on the other side, offering him a smile before opening the first of her papers and getting her pen ready to circle.

The first one was mainly care work and cleaning which, although she would consider, wasn't the direction she was hoping to go in. She circled a couple of possibilities, though - mainly the ones that didn't require any experience and had an immediate start - before moving onto the next.

"Looking for a job?" the man asked with a gravelly voice that sounded like he had spent many years smoking.

"Yes, I am actually," she said, glancing at him before returning to her paper, scanning the next page and feeling disappointed when nearly every job required experience in fields she didn't have. Fishing, cooking, accounting - nothing she thought she had a hope of getting. There was an advert for a dog-walker, which she circled; it wasn't a full time income, but perhaps she could gain a little money that way, while she tried to find something.

"I hear they're looking for someone over at Greenway," he said, raising a hand and pointing in the distance to a building over the water.

"Greenway? As in Agatha's Christie's house?"

He nodded. "Tour guide or some such, I was told. Might be worth checking out."

"It definitely will be! Thank you, I really appreciate it."

She tried to control her expectations as she shook the man's hand, learning that his name was John. After all, there might not be a job there... or they might need experience. But there was something about the suggestion that made her feel excited, and it had been a long time since she had felt excited about a job prospect. Maybe there could be more to a job than just making enough money to pay the rent and endless bills.

She considered waiting until the next day to go and check out the possibility, but was too impatient. Lunch, a change into something that would make a great first impression, and then she could figure out how one even got over to Greenway. Even if the job prospect was a bust, she would still get to see the home of a writer she had always loved - that was worth an afternoon, surely.

John moved away to get on with whatever it was he did with his days - she suspected something outdoors, with that overcoat - and as the sky threatened to drop the rain it had been storing for the last few balmy days, Beth skipped off to get a few essentials that she had not yet had time to buy: milk, bread, cheese and toilet roll. She had stolen a toilet roll from Lee the previous night, but that did not seem like a sensible way to continue with living her life. As long as she budgeted enough to get the ferry over to Greenway, and the entrance fee if things didn't go to plan, she thought she'd be okay.

Things had to work out. This had to be a sign, surely

- she had her flat, and now a lead on a job - plus a newspaper that she hadn't yet perused. The heavens opened and as the rain filled the dry streets and emptied them of people, Beth ran back to the flat, already planning what she could wear to impress whoever she would meet at Greenway...

There was a crush in the shop when she entered, probably thanks to the sudden downpour, and as she tried to get through to the little side door that led up to her flat, she heard Sam shout.

"Hey, Bethany-"

"It's Beth!" she shouted back.

"Beth. I'm snowed under here, Jenny's rung in sick and I can't keep on top of all of this. Want a few hours work? I'll pay you!"

She contemplated her options. On one hand, she wanted to go to Greenway right now. On the other, she needed the money - and she could always do that tomorrow. Or later on in the day. Her financial situation certainly was dire...

"Go on then," she said, getting through the crowd to get behind the counter and grabbing an apron from where he pointed.

"Can you wash up to start with? Then get chips in the fryer - fill the basket, put it in, be careful because it's boiling and I don't have time to take you to A&E."

"Charming," Beth said, rolling up her sleeves and getting on with it. It was all money, after all.

The three hours she worked in the shop that afternoon were possibly the most physical hours of work she had ever done, and she was surprised by just how tired she was when the rush finally ended and Sam became a little more polite and thanked her for stepping in. He opened the till and handed her £30, which she felt was well-earned.

"I'm job hunting at the minute," she said, folding up the apron carefully. "So if you get desperate again, I might be able to help."

"Cheers," he said, grabbing a can of coke and swigging loudly from it. "Do you want fish and chips? On the house? I do appreciate you stepping in, I know just because you live here doesn't mean I should just pull you in to the madness!"

"Don't worry, I'm quite good at saying no," Beth said with a smile, but took him up on the offer of fish and chips. It was too late now to go to Greenway, and she was starving, having missed her planned lunch of a cheese sandwich. This was definitely preferable, and as she dumped her bag of groceries on the kitchen counter upstairs, she couldn't wait to tuck in.

She chose to sit by the window again, watching the view from her window as she ate the delicious battered cod, in spite of the fact that rain poured down the windows. She could still see the boats no longer bobbing but rocking energetically on the disturbed waters. People were a scarcity, with the weather having pushed them all into shops, cafés, pubs and certainly fish and chip shops - or sending them scurrying home.

A man in a green coat was tethering up a boat, and she wondered if it were John, the helpful soul who'd suggested she try looking across the water for a job. He certainly was suffering the worst of the weather.

She knew she should make the most of the time, but for a while it was nice to just sit there, letting a sleepiness from a large meal and some hard work wash over her, watching the rain pour down the windows and letting her eyes drift slowly closed...

CHAPTER ELEVEN

Bright and early the next morning - well, Beth felt bright, the weather not so much - she headed out of the flat dressed in a blue dress with matching flats, hoping she looked smart enough without being out of place at a historical building. She'd done some research, after her impromptu nap the previous evening, and found the ferry was the quickest way to get over the water - and she felt a thrill at the thought, for she couldn't remember the last time she'd taken a passenger ferry. It was a short walk to where she needed to get on, and the ferry was busy with what she presumed were commuters, working on the other side of the water.

Beth found a spot next to the rail, where she could look out across the water and take in the moving scenery, as the ferry departed and slowly chugged to its destination. Out on a boat, which rose slightly in the waves coming from the ferry, was the man in the green coat again; she seemed to be seeing him everywhere. He had a flat cap on, and she raised a hand in greeting, and thought he waved back - although she would be surprised if he could recognise her at this distance. It was his distinctive green coat, after all, that she recognised - and she wasn't in anything that could identify her.

She'd left her fine blonde hair loose that morning, and it blew around her face as they moved, making Beth feel like she were out at sea, instead of the reality of not being that far from her own flat. She let the others off before she followed, smoothing down her hair and checking her appearance in a window before heading up the path and away from the water. The air felt close, and she wondered if they might have a thunderstorm by the end of the day.

It was a narrow single-track road up towards the house, and she followed the brown signs pointing out the local attraction. There were a few other people further ahead, but it wasn't too busy; it was a little before the season started, for one, and the weather was not as pleasant as it had been the last few days. The heat was still surprising though, and as she reached the top of the hill, Beth regretted the decision to leave her shoulder-length hair down, as it felt as though it was sticking to the back of her neck in the humidity.

At the entrance to the grounds she gave herself a moment, leaning by one of the grand pillars, to catch her breath and try to fix her appearance as best as she could, using her fingers as a comb and the window of the little stone building by the pillar as a mirror.

Another long walk down a driveway, through grounds that she thought she might explore at a later date, and then there it was in front of her; a large, imposing white building, with elegant columns and full of windows to spy out of. The grey clouds above gave it an ominous feeling, but Beth just lapped that up - it was an air of mystery, an air of possibility that excited rather than concerned her.

"Hello dear, welcome to Greenway, home of mystery and intrigue!" A white-haired lady greeted her at the payment desk, and Beth grinned at the words.

"Hello!"

"Just one adult's entrance?"

"Well, yes, I would love to see the building, but I also had a question. I heard from a gentleman in Dartmouth that there might be a job available here, and I wanted to see if that was true!"

The lady smiled and put down her ticket book. "Well, you're not misinformed, miss-"

"Davis. Beth Davis."

"Beth. I'm Tanya. We're looking for a tour guide, for the season mainly, although it could continue past that, depending on the staffing situation come September. Have you done any tour guide work before?"

Ah, here was the issue. Experience - it always came up. "No, I haven't," Beth said, deciding to go with honest but enthusiastic. "But I've always been a massive Agatha Christie fan, and I'm a quick learner of facts - and I just moved to Dartmouth this week!"

Tanya smiled, and Beth hoped that was a good sign. "Well, experience isn't essential, although it certainly helps. Let's take a walk through the house, shall we, and get to know each other?" Beth nodded keenly, taking a surreptitious sip from her sadly warm water bottle and following her through the turnstile.

"As you might be aware, this was a holiday home for

Agatha Christie and her family," she said, as they entered a large living room with bookcases forming a large part of the wall. "Things have been left as they were then, filled with all sorts of artifacts from their travels and things the family collected. What we need here is someone to take the booked tours around. Someone who can learn about all the features and quirks, and share their enthusiasm with those who've paid for tours - as well as touring the gardens."

"That sounds amazing," Beth said, reading a page open in a scrap book filled with memories of Christie's childhood.

Tanya smiled. "So you just moved to Dartmouth?"

She nodded. "From Exeter."

"On your own?"

"Yep. My sister and her family live in Totnes though, so I'm not completely stranded!"

"That's nice. And what work have you done previously?"

She listed her most recent jobs, but didn't go back too far - she didn't want to put the lady off with such an extensive list of jobs. She knew it made her look a little flaky - but her days of constant job-hopping were, she felt, in her past; and besides, this was probably only temporary. Still, what a great job to do for three months or so.

"A lot of experience! How old are you, if you don't mind me asking?"

"Twenty-eight," Beth said, her smile slightly nervous.

"And an Agatha Christie fan from since I could read properly!"

Tanya's smile broadened a little at that one. "And you could start immediately, if you were offered the job?"

"Yes, as soon as you liked. I have a car, and live right near the ferry, too, so I'm flexible."

"Okay, well, let's go to the back room and look at some paperwork - but it all sounds good to me!"

Beth felt her heart soar.

It would all work out...

"Well, Elizabeth Davis, I'm very glad you came in this morning!" Tanya said after Beth had filled in the third form. "I'd be very happy for you to come and work here - providing your references come through all right from your previous employment, of course." Beth couldn't wipe the smile from her face. She was pretty confident that her references would be good - after all, although she'd felt like she was going nowhere, she'd always turned up and always been praised for doing a good job. And although this opportunity was only temporary, it still felt like something that she could really sink her teeth into, something she could be passionate about.

"I'm so glad I came, too," Beth said, shaking Tanya's hand. "So, do I wait to hear from you?"

"Let's just set a start date, shall we? And then I'll give you a ring if there's any issues. How does Monday sound?"

"Perfect."

Tanya said goodbye, leaving her free to wander the

house at her leisure, and a pleasant hour or so passed as she explored the different rooms, learning as much as she could soak in - not just for the job she would be starting, but for her own interest too. These were places and objects that had inspired someone who had filled many of Beth's evenings as a child and a teenager, and she couldn't help but feel inspired herself. Inspired to make something of the opportunity, even if she wasn't quite sure what.

The grounds were next, and she discovered a sight which took her breath away. Passing a brick wall, she came across a secluded fountain, surround by an array of ferns and greenery that fanned out around the cascading water, with moss filling in any gaps, making the whole area a lush green. It felt truly magical; as though fairies could live there,unknown beneath the umbrellas of ferns, weaving their magic on the inhabitants of the house and gardens.

Outside the walled garden, Beth leant back on a wooden bench, and pulled out her phone.

It was time.

Three rings were all that she had before the line was picked up; very little time to get her words together, but then she thought that if she had time to think, she'd just decide not to do this - and it needed to be done.

"Hello?"

"Hi mum."

"Elizabeth, hello, I wasn't expecting to hear from you today."

Beth sighed; it was always the way with her mother.

She knew it wasn't meant in any cruel way, but the words certainly made her feel like her phone call was unwanted, not just unexpected.

"I've got news," Beth said, jumping straight in at the deep-end, response be damned.

"Oh?"

A deep breath, then the words came tumbling from her mouth: "I've moved. To Dartmouth."

"Sorry... you've moved to Dartmouth? When?"

"Two days ago."

"And... and... was this planned? Or is this just another one of your spontaneous mistakes?"

"Not planned, and not a mistake. I don't want to argue mum, I really don't - but I don't want my own mum to not know where I'm living. So there it is - I've moved to Dartmouth, I'm only fifteen minutes from Lee, and I just got a job."

"I don't know what to say, Elizabeth..."

"Say: Congratulations on the job! Or that you'll visit soon. I'm happy about this, mum - I'd had enough of going nowhere. I needed something to change."

"Well, then... I hope it works out for you." It was strained, but the words were positive, and Beth decided to take them in that way.

"Thanks mum. I'd better run - we'll catch up properly soon."

It was on the way to the ferry that the heavens opened once more, but it did not stop Beth from skipping down the hill. She couldn't wait for things to start; for her life to truly begin.

◆ ◆ ◆

It was a dark and stormy night, she wrote, then put a line straight through it. It was a cliché, she knew, and sounded more like a children's story than whatever it was she was trying to write.

Rain streamed down the windows as though the world was mourning this loss, and wind buffeted the old glass panes, making Adelaide shiver despite the warmth of the fire. This night, surely, was the night when they would find out who had murdered her father-in-law. This night, full of misery and despair, must be the night when he was finally apprehended...

She glanced back at what she had written in the leather-bound journal she had purchased when she was only visiting Dartmouth with Lee, and smiled. She had never written creatively before - well, not since she was in school and had no choice - but she found she was pleased with the words that were coming out. She had no plot, no plan, just the inspiration from that view, that house, and the vision of Adelaide, sat by a fire in a rickety old building, wearing a faded red dress framed in brocade, waiting for a killer to be caught.

She had been desperate to write for the whole journey back, the words building in her mind as they traversed the disturbed waters and as she dashed home to cracks of thunder. She was sure lightening would soon be upon them, and she knew that she wanted to be safe in her flat with a cup of tea once that happened.

And so here she was, facing out to the miserable, dramatic weather, a cup of tea to one side, a pen in her hand, and a whole world ahead of her that she could create. She felt as though the electricity that was shooting from the charcoal skies was running through her fingertips, and it was the most alive she had ever felt.

This was what she'd wanted, she realised, when she'd upped and left everything she knew. Something that would truly get her excited about her life - and as small as it might seem to others, this was making her excited. This job, this flat, this notebook: it thrilled her.

CHAPTER TWELVE

Monday morning rolled around with a blue sky speckled with occasional white clouds. Beth had spent the night before agonising over what to wear, and had finally settled on a blue button-down dress covered with sailing boats. It felt appropriate to the setting, at least, and she felt as though she looked professional in it.

She waited for the ferry with a few other people, choosing to take the earlier one of the two options, and with her travel mug of tea in one hand she leant against the railings, watching the gulls swooping over the water.

"Good morning," a gruff voice came behind her, and she jumped out of her daydreaming state before realising who it was.

"John!" she said with a wide grin. "Good morning! And thank you so much for the tip the other day - I got the job!"

"I thought you might have done," he said, heading down the steps towards the boats. "Good luck!"

It felt like a great start to the day. The ferry was perfectly on time, and as it chugged along the water, she felt pleased she'd put her hair into a more business-like bun today - it would save her looking bedraggled before she even got there.

She huffed and puffed her way up the hill, having forgotten the distance she had to walk the other side, but decided to look on the positive: a few weeks of walking like this and she would be so much fitter than she was at the minute. She'd spent far too long sat at a desk.

Despite the hard work getting there, she looked at her watch as she reached the pillars announcing the grand estate and was pleased to find she was still twenty minutes early. She decided to take a few minutes to compose herself on a bench, finish off her tea, and take a few deep breaths. Letting her eyes flutter closed, she focused on breathing in, and out, drinking in the peacefulness that surrounded her. A few nerves fluttered in her stomach, but it was excitement, more than anything, that made her feel a little restless.

Eighteen minutes early. How early could you be on your first day? She didn't want to get in the way… perhaps ten minutes? And so she pulled out the leather-bound notebook from her handbag, put the pen to paper and let the words that kept filling her head flow out.

It had not been a simple marriage, even before murder arrived on their doorstep. Three years of matrimony, but it certainly had not been wedded bliss. There was the fact that her husband had been chosen for her by her father; then the fact that he was ten years older than she. But she thought she could have got past both of those facts, if it were not for the third: the fact that he was undoubtedly in love with another.

Three years of being married to someone who was polite, and kind, and wholly invested in another person had made Adelaide's heart feel as though it had shrivelled to the size of a prune. She had once had childish dreams of falling in love, of marrying for love - and, even once she was married, of falling in love with her husband, as the characters in her favourite novels always seemed to - but that hope was now lost to her.

And now he was in mourning for his father, and she felt terrified to step outside her front door in case the perpetrator had some vendetta against their family - and things were so much worse than they had ever been before.

Suddenly, Beth looked at her watch and jumped up out of the bench in shock. Never mind eighteen minutes - time had run away with her and she had less than three before she would become late. She shoved the notebook and pen back in her bag, took one final deep breath and hurried to the front desk to meet Tanya.

"Good morning, Beth!" She greeted her like an old friend, with an easy smile and clasp of her hands. "Great to see you again, and your references were brilliant, so we've got a busy season ahead of us!"

"I can't wait to get started," Beth said truthfully.

"Well, it's going to be a lot of reading to begin with, I'm afraid - to familiarise yourself with everything we have here. Then hopefully we can get you out on the floor with another guide tomorrow, and on your own by Wednesday, if that all sounds okay with you!"

"Definitely," Beth said. Being made to read about this

beautiful house and its contents for a day hardly seemed like a chore - in fact, the day sped by so fast that Tanya had to come into the little back room to remind her to have some lunch and take a break.

It seemed there were four members of staff working at a time at the property, as well as a gardener to tend the grounds, and they took lunches at different times so they had enough staff on the floor. However, as Beth was essentially extra that day, she took lunch with another member of staff, and as they unpacked their sandwiches (Beth's was simply cheese, as that was all she'd had in), Beth was pleased to note that the lady in a sky-blue dress covered in daisies was closer to her own age.

"I'm Laila," she said, as they began to eat. "I've been here for two years, every holiday while I'm doing my degree."

"I'm Beth. First day!"

"I'd presumed!"

"What are you studying?"

"Archaeology," she said. "I didn't go to uni when I was younger so here I am, thirty-two and doing a degree. My friends think I'm mad, but it was the decision that felt right for me, you know?"

"I totally understand that!" Beth said, with a grin, deciding to confide her secrets in this new acquaintance. "I moved to Dartmouth on a complete whim, on a feeling that I got when I was down here visiting my sister for a week. Felt I needed a change and, well, here I am!"

Laila had just taken a large bite of her sandwich and

took a moment to respond. "Wow. That's brave!"

"Or stupid!" Beth said with a laugh.

"I think," said Beth, as she and Lee sat in Lee's garden, drinking orange juice and soaking up the sunshine that weekend, "That I'm writing a novel."

"A novel?"

"Well, I'm writing, and I feel like that's what it is! Whether I'll finish it, who knows, but I gotta say that I'm loving it at the minute!"

"That's amazing, Beth," Lee said, watching her daughter on a play mat in front of them. She occasionally crawled off at great speed, and Lee would dash off to stop her getting into the hedges or onto the gravel.

"It's this place, honestly - it makes me feel inspired in a way that I never have been. Not just with the writing, but with getting up in the morning, going to work..."

"The new job's going well then?"

"It really is. I'm doing tours on my own now, I remember almost everything, I'm in beautiful places all the time..."

Lee watched her sister for several moments before speaking again. "I'm so pleased for you, Beth. It seems like everything really did work out!"

"Well, I don't want to say I told you so, but..."

"Yeah, yeah, you were right!" They both laughed, causing Holly to look up at them. She made a sound then, as she watched Lee, a sound that made Lee and Beth glance at one another and then back at the baby.

"Mamam."

"Did she-"

"Did that sound like-"

"I think so!"

"Clever girl!" Lee said, picking up her daughter and swooping her in the air. "Mama! Mama!"

CHAPTER THIRTEEN

Although Beth's days became a routine of writing, going to work, the occasional evening (although not late-night!) trip to the sea and seeing her sister, somehow she did not feel that dragging sense of monotony that had plagued her in her old job. She reasoned that it had only been a few weeks, and that this might change, but as the end of July approached, and Beth could get up the hill without getting out of breath, she found she still looked forward to work every single day - and how many people could truly say that!

It was an ordinary Tuesday, a light breeze in the air, a day that seemed no different than the twenty or so that had preceded it. Beth sat on a bench waiting for the ferry, as had become her custom, and scribbled away in her notebook at the story that was now far greater than a few paragraphs long.

Adelaide had spent some time dong detective work of her own, both to while away the hours and in the hopes of finding something that had been missed by one of the many men who were involved in the case. She did not tell anyone this; they would have laughed at the idea of a woman being capable of some sleuthing.

One night, when rain once again battered the windows

and her husband was mysteriously late home, she'd found a letter hidden in a between the stonework of the living room. She'd been almost excited at its discovery, convinced it must be something of interest to the case, but when she had read it, it had only served to further batter her poor, withered heart.

'There can be no divorce in this family. You married her and you will have children with her. Keep as many mistresses as you wish but do not utter the word divorce again.'

"Every day I see you writing in that thing," John's voice said from a spot against the rails where, unbeknown to Beth he had been standing for some time. "Can I ask what you're writing?"

Beth blushed, adding a full stop to the end of a sentence and meeting his eye. "It's a novel," she admitted, something which she had told only Lee.

"What sort of novel?"

"A murder mystery."

"Ahh." He rested the end of his pipe between his fingers, and Beth glanced at it, realising she had never seen someone actually smoking a pipe before. Perhaps that was something that could be added to her novel... "Taking inspiration from your work, eh?"

"I think so," Beth said. "The words just seem to be in my mind, fighting to get out - oh, there's the ferry. Sorry John, I'll have to run!"

"Keep up the writing!" he shouted as she dashed past a crowd of tourists to reach the ferry, and although they were the words of someone she didn't know all that well, somehow they cheered her. Perhaps she could tell other people what she was writing - perhaps, one day, she could actually let them read it!

◆ ◆ ◆

The first tour group started at ten, and once they had paid Laila who was on the counter that morning, Beth ushered them into the living room to start her spiel.

She was three minutes in when she felt an uncomfortable feeling as though she were being watched very intently. Of course, she *was* being watched, by eight pairs of interested eyes - but this feeling was more pronounced, and she tried to look at the faces of those watching her to figure out where the feeling originated - without, of course, getting distracted from the information she was giving. An elderly couple stood on her left, nodding along with what she was saying but certainly not staring; then a family of four, with two younger children that were barely listening to a word she said. An older woman stood to their right, with kind brown eyes and a smile, and then-

And then she did stumble over her words. It was so unexpected, so jarring - like a bolt of electricity going through her.

It was him.

She cleared her throat, apologised, and finished what she needed to say, all the while fully aware that a man who had seen her swimming - and possibly nearly drowning - in her underwear, a man who had possession of an item of her underwear, was staring directly at her. It made the blood rise to her cheeks, and it took every ounce of focus she had in her to finish the speech before she could let them roam the room for a few minutes in peace.

He didn't come directly towards her; instead he accompanied the woman with the kind brown eyes around the room, while Beth surveyed them all, judging when it was time to move on . She couldn't approach him - it was mortifying. If he pretended he didn't know who she was, she decided she would do the same; after all, there was a chance that he didn't know who she was. Perhaps he didn't remember, or didn't recognise her fully clothed and not bathed in moonlight.

The thought made her blush even harder.

As they approached the vase standing directly to her left, she felt the hairs on her arms prickle and stand on end. Her breathing was shallow, and she couldn't focus on anything but this mysterious man who might or might not have a clue who she was.

"I think I have something belonging to you," he said, in the softest possible whisper - but she heard.

Aware that she needed to remain professional, at least to the rest of the tour group, she turned to one side, hoping her speech would be more hidden that way. "Perhaps you shouldn't go stealing people's...clothes," she said, feeling a lot more flustered than she hoped she sounded.

"Add 'don't leave your underwear with strangers' to the list of things *you* shouldn't be doing," he said, after checking that the woman - who Beth assumed was his mother - wasn't close enough to hear.

"It wasn't on purpose! A gentleman wouldn't have mentioned it."

"Who said I'm a gentleman? But if you're swimming tonight, I can return it to you..."

She was a little embarrassed that he'd kept it, but there was something very alluring about the idea of seeing him again, seeing him in that water, feeling the water droplets on his skin...

She tried to stop the direction her thoughts were headed, but it wasn't easy with this tension crackling between her and such a handsome, grumpy man.

"Ten o'clock? Same place?"

"I'll be there," he said, and then Beth realised how long they had been in that room, and quickly ushered them on for the rest of the much pacier tour.

It was at the end of the tour, as she led the guests out into the sunny grounds and said goodbye, that she allowed herself to look at him again. He was talking to his mother, and she watched as his chiseled jaw moved, a smattering of stubble covering it. He was tall - so much taller than she was - and his dark hair looked almost black, even under the bright sunshine they were enjoying. Even in a polo shirt and dark jeans she could see the outlines of muscles in his arms.

"Thank you for a wonderful tour." She was forced to stop staring at him when his companion addressed her. "I've been going on at my Caspian for years to bring me here, and I'm so glad he did. You're very knowledgeable dear, you must be quite experienced at this tour guide business!"

"Thank you so much," Beth said with a smile. "I'm so glad you had a good time. I've actually only been here for a few weeks, but I'm very enthusiastic about the place and its history!"

"Well, I would never have been able to tell. Wasn't she wonderful, Cas?"

"Very enlightening," he agreed in a dry voice, but when Beth forced herself to meet his dark brown eyes she saw a smile on his face that was reflected in them.

"Well, we must be on our way, I'm sure he's got time to take his old mother out for lunch before he has to dash off to work. All work and no play makes for a dull person!"

"Very dull," Beth agreed, smiling back and trying not to laugh. She watched as they walked down the hill, mother holding onto son's arm, and it was only once they reached the very bottom of the hill that she tore her eyes away and disappeared back inside for the next round.

She knew her reaction to him had been strange, but there was no time to dwell on that now. And nor would there be that evening, when she had somehow agreed to another late night swim with the handsome, mysterious Caspian...

CHAPTER FOURTEEN

She wore a bikini this time, and took a towel - no-one could say that Beth Davis did not learn from her mistakes. It had been another gloriously sunny day, and she hoped the water would be as warm and inviting as she remembered - and that he would show up. Perhaps it had all been a joke...

She found it hard to wait until closer to ten to drive to the beach, and tried not to over-analyse the thrill she was feeling about this meeting. She told herself it was just because it was an act of rebellion - a late night swim, meeting with a handsome stranger, retrieving her bra. Nothing more was going to happen...

She was on the road by twenty to ten, unable to focus on the writing that had consumed her for the last few weeks. In the day time, the beaches were packed now that the summer holidays were in full swing and Devon had become the tourist haven it was known to be. But by this time in the evening, as the sky faded from reds and oranges to blues and blacks, there were very few people still there. A glow and a column of smoke in the distance with a group of what looked like teenagers huddled around it to one end; at another, a slightly hunched over man throwing a ball repeatedly for two large and bounding dogs - and that was it.

For a few quiet, undisturbed moments, she watched as the waves gently lapped in and out, dampening the shingle and then softly retreating, taking a few smaller pebbles and grains of sand with them. Then a figure strode towards the spot where she had taken off her dress and shoes those few short weeks ago, and she hurried down to meet him.

He was already in his swimming trunks - she presumed he had changed behind that rock again, although she hadn't seen him as she surveyed the beach - and on hearing her approach, he turned to face her, holding one strap of her black, lacy bra between his thumb and finger tips.

"No need to flash my underwear to the world," she said, snatching it from his hands and stuffing it into her handbag.

He raised his eyebrows and flashed a smile. "Says you!"

She blushed, and dipped her head.

"Coming for a swim?"

"I've got a towel and everything."

"I was willing to share again..." he said, then took off towards the water, gliding straight in without pausing to let his body acclimatise. She was pleased he'd gone in first; it gave her a chance to take her dress off without being observed, and to hide her body in the depths of the water as it reflected the dying rays of the sunset.

The water was cool, but pleasantly so, and she was soon submerged to her knees, then her stomach, all the while watching his repetitive strokes backwards and forwards through the gentle waves.

Then he stopped, and looked back.

"Are you coming?"

With a deep breath, she submerged her shoulders and began to move through the water with a slow breast stroke that kept her head bobbing above the water, her hair in its bun occasionally grazing the surface.

When she reached him, she was surprised to find he hadn't simply swum off, but was stood there, watching her swim.

"You're very fast," she said, feeling uncomfortable in the silence as they looked at each other, water up to their waists, shoulders glistening.

"Lots of practice," he said. "You could get faster, if you wanted to."

"Is that an insult to my current speed?"

"No, I mean-"

"Relax, I'm joking," Beth said, pleased to have flustered him at least a tenth of the amount he seemed to fluster her.

"I didn't think you'd come."

"I thought you might be joking."

"Why did you come?"

Beth ducked her shoulders back under, not wanting to reach the level of cold she'd somehow reached the last time she'd been in this situation and let herself get distracted by good looks and piercing eyes.

"I don't know. The thrill of a late night swim?"

"You've not been back since that night."

Inside, there was a very immature part of her that was screaming out: He noticed! He noticed!

"I've been taking earlier swims. Realised drowning when there was no-one else around probably wasn't the best idea..." she admitted, feeling even shorter with him towering above her as she allowed her body to be submerged in the water. "You'll get cold if you stay out of the water that long - trust me."

He blinked, then ducked his shoulders too, until they were the same height and somehow - and she didn't know whose movement had caused it - even closer together.

"I've never met anyone who strips off to their underwear and swims when everyone else is at home in bed."

She couldn't follow his train of thought, so just focussed on answering the questions he threw at her - although that one wasn't particularly a question. She shrugged, and went to run a hand through her hair before remembering it was in a bun and not loose for her to fiddle with. "I like to break the rules," she said. "I like to be spontaneous."

"You've not been here very long, have you?"

"About a month," she said. "Another spontaneous decision."

She could have sworn she could feel heat radiating from him through the water - or maybe it was coming from her.

"I can't remember the last time I made a spontaneous decision," he said, their eyes not leaving each other's, as the sun disappeared behind the horizon.

"You go swimming in the ocean at ten o'clock at night! That seems pretty bold to me."

"Never spontaneous, though," he said. "I do this every night, from April to October."

"Disciplined."

"If I tell you I want to kiss you, does that take away from it being a spontaneous decision?"

Her eyes froze for a moment, and she could find no words to answer this sudden declaration. Instead, she simply shook her head, and took a step forward in the dark waters.

His hands moved slowly, painfully slowly, through the water, before resting on her waist, and she gasped at the contact, that sudden burst of heat in the cold surroundings, as he pulled her closer to him, and then they were standing, and her chest was pressed against his, and there was heat radiating from everywhere...

"You are a very intriguing woman," he said, his lips hovering above hers, her neck bent so she could still look into those eyes.

"You make the words disappear from my head," she

said, unaware of how honest she was being, because all she could think of was his lips, the feel of his heart beating in his chest - or maybe that was hers, they were so close it was hard to tell - the stubble that she could feel under her fingertips as she allowed her hands to reach up and touch that perfect face.

And then he kissed her.

There was a saltiness to the kiss, and there was a gentleness that she had not expected. She let her arms wrap round his neck as the kiss deepened, let him hold the weight of her as their lips moved together; as the fireworks filled her mind and made her abandon all sense of place and time. They were kneeling in the water now, and his fingers were caught in her hair, and the only thing that could have separated them was a bolt of lightening. His tongue met hers and a noise that she did not recognise escaped from her throat, a longing and a hunger that had not been awoken in a very long time.

She wasn't sure who finally broke the kiss, or how long they'd been there, but when they eventually separated their lips, both were breathing heavily and neither could find words for several minutes.

Slowly, they untangled themselves, Beth wincing a little as his fingers caught on a few strands of hair, and put a little space between themselves - although occasionally a hand floated through the water and brushed a thigh, or an arm, and another frisson of electric passed through that calm water.

"That was definitely spontaneous," Beth said, when her breath had finally come under her control.

Caspian grinned, and she thought he might even be blushing, although it was obscured by the ever-darkening sky.

"I think I might like spontaneous," he said.

"I think spontaneous was pretty... explosive," she responded, trying to gauge whether he had felt that same ferocity of sensation. It had only been six weeks or so since she had last been kissed, by the ginger youth with the wisdom that night in the club, but the difference between the two kisses was phenomenal. She had forgotten what it could feel like - or perhaps she had never known. Had she ever been kissed to the point of her legs feeling like they might disintegrate beneath her? It was a good job the sea took most of her weight, else she thought she might be a heap on the floor.

"Explosive - that's definitely one way to put it."

"I've interrupted your regularly scheduled swim," she said, grinning at his agreement.

"I feel like I've had a pretty good work out," he said, and there was that dry sense of humour again - but this time it made Beth laugh, and give him a gentle shove backwards. She was surprised that he actually lost his footing, splashing slightly as he fought to right himself, and she took advantage of the moment: "Last one back to shore loses!"

He won, of course he did, despite her underhand tactics and head start. He had the experience, that was for sure, and he overtook her smoothly, splashing a little more than she felt was necessary as he passed her.

He was towel drying his hair when she finally stepped out of the water, feeling less self-conscious this time about being in her bikini - which was the same colour as the underwear set she'd been wearing anyway, but did at least soak in less water.

"What do I win?" he asked with a cheeky grin, as she pulled her own towel out of her bag. "Or are you just going to throw your underwear at me again?"

"You are insufferable!" she said. "You know full well that I left it there by accident."

"Seems a little convenient to me," he said. "I think it was all some great plan…"

"What, to lure you back to the beach and kiss you senseless in the sea?"

He grinned. "Well, look what happened."

"I don't think I'm the mastermind here…"

"This was not planned," he insisted, drying off the water droplets that clung to the hair on his chest. She found her gaze wandering from his eyes, out of her control… "Spontaneity, remember?"

"So," Beth said, feeling she was as dry as she was going to get without taking off her bikini - which was certainly *not* happening this time - and throwing her dress over the top. "Do you think we'll *spontaneously* meet again?"

"Well, this is the third time it's happened…"

Silently, Beth disagreed - this had most definitely been organised, even if only through a whispered comment - but she didn't want to take the impulsive moment away from him. And she wanted her question answered.

"Say I was to be at the bar at The Fort in Dartmouth at seven o'clock on Saturday, do you think we might happen to run into each other?" he asked, pausing in his towel ministrations to watch her reaction.

"I think there would be a good chance of that happening," she said.

"So, can I claim my prize?"

Beth looked confused. "Prize?"

"For coming first in the race. There has to be a prize…"

"Just the joy of not being the loser which, unfortunately, I am," she said, with a hand on one hip.

"You don't look like a loser to me," he said, taking three quick steps towards her. "But since I am the winner… one kiss seems a fair prize, don't you think?"

"It depends on your definition of one kiss," Beth said, feeling a little breathless at the thought, at his proximity. "I mean, back there, in the sea…"

"The explosion?"

"Uh-huh. Can that really count as one kiss?"

"You mean we need to think about length," he took another step closer, "And intensity…" His hand hovered at her waist, making her ache for the contact, and any clever thoughts swam clean out of her mind as she nodded her head.

"Yes," she said, not even knowing what she was saying yes to - his words, the kiss, him - but she wanted him to claim that prize. He could have as many kisses as he wanted if they made her feel like *that*.

He pressed his lips to hers for a fraction of a second, then pulled them away. "One kiss," he said, and although even that brief contact had made the fireworks start fizzing in her mind, she felt bereft at the loss of another earth-shattering moment.

She almost said something. Almost begged for him to give her more. Almost shouted at him for sticking to the silly rules she seemed to be creating in her flirtatious words - and then she pressed her lips closed and remembered that leaving him wanting more was never a bad strategy. Even if she wanted to grab hold of him...

"I'll see you around then," he said, taking a step backwards, and after looking at her for a moment longer, Caspian turned on his heel and jogged away down that unknown path.

Beth felt like she needed to sit down. No, scratch that, she felt as though she needed a lie down in a darkened room with a stiff drink. Never could she remember someone affecting her to the point where she wasn't sure if she had control of her words, her mind, or even the movement of her legs anymore. Never had she wanted a kiss to go on longer so desperately... Never had she been so thrilled by a simple kiss.

But, as she drove home without really paying attention to the directions, she realised there had been nothing simple about that kiss. That kiss, in the middle of the ocean, with the sun setting behind them, was the sort of kiss that only happened once in a lifetime. And she would treasure the memory of her impulsiveness.

Sleep didn't come easily that night, as she replayed the evening in her head, and thought forwards to their planned meeting on Saturday. Was it a date? She supposed so, although things were not so clearly defined as that - which made it all the more exciting. She was desperate to tell someone about it, but telling Lee of her night-time water adventures seemed a little premature... and if Lee judged her, she might well question her own sanity, which was not something she wanted to do. So she messaged the person who she knew would happily climb into her crazy little bubble without an ounce of judgment.

I found the fireworks!

Jasmine replied almost instantly, which made Beth laugh to herself in the darkness of her bedroom: it was nearly midnight, and if it had been about anything else but a boy she was sure Jas would have ignored it until the next day - and probably forgotten even then, until Beth had reminded her.

OMG. Need details!! Knew there'd be a man on the scene before long!

Too many details to share, but fireworks were definitely exploding!

Phone call tomorrow evening - we'll have wine and share everything. Jx

CHAPTER FIFTEEN

Ten minutes before she had to leave for work, she was surprised to hear a knock on her front door. Considering that, in order to get to her front door, you had to come through the fish and chip shop, it was not something that had ever happened before. Post for her - bills, mainly - went to the shop too, and so she had no idea who could possibly be rapping on her door so early in the morning.

When she opened the door, her mouth dropped slightly, and she only had a second to recover before the woman pushed her way in and closed the door behind her.

"Good morning, Elizabeth."

"Mum. Hi. What are you doing here?" She got over her initial shock and reached over to give her mum - who she saw was ominously equipped with a roller suitcase - a hug.

"I thought I'd visit my daughters, since they both decided to up and move to the middle of nowhere - although you failed to tell me you lived above a chip shop."

"It didn't seem relevant," she said, glancing up at the clock on the wall. "Mum, I'm sorry, I've got to dash to work right now. How did you even manage to get up here, anyway?"

"The boy downstairs knew what was good for him and let me in the door at the bottom. Are you going to complain about me seeing my daughter?"

"No, mum, of course not. Look, why don't you go over to Lee's, she should be at home, and I'll come round after work? Are you staying?"

"That was the plan, although I guess I'll have to check into a hotel."

"Stay with Lee, mum, I'm sure she'd love you to," Beth said, inwardly not so sure she was saying the right thing. "I'd offer here but I only have the sofa..."

"If I can ever find that cottage of hers, I guess I'll do that."

Beth did her best to give her mother hurried directions as they walked down the steps, giving Sam a sharp glare behind her mum's back.

"I've got to run, mum, or I'll miss the ferry over and be late. I'll see you this evening - love you!"

She dashed off without looking back, and only when she was safely on the ferry did she pull out her phone.

Mum's in town, sent her your way, sorry!! Be warned, she has a suitcase. X

The shocked face symbols that came back made Beth laugh, and although she felt a little guilty for landing Lee with their mother for the day, she let the feeling float away and stood leaning against the rail, feeling the wind blowing through her hair and letting images of last night's kiss wash over her yet again.

It was only as she got in her car to drive to Lee's after a busy day at work that she remembered the promised phone call with Jasmine, and before setting off, pulled out her phone to fire off a text.

My mother turned up, so the phone call will have to be late-ish - say ten? I'll need the wine by then! B xx

Perfect - so long as you don't forget any steamy details!!

Oh, they're ingrained on my mind ;)

She laughed at the exchange as she drove out of Dartmouth, with the windows down and the local radio on, and sang to her heart's content to every repetitive pop song that was played.

"I just don't understand what your plan is, Elizabeth," Tina said for the millionth time.

"There isn't a plan, mum - thanks James, this is delicious," she added, tucking in to the risotto James had served them.

"It is very good, James," Tina said, before turning back to Beth. "But there has to be some sort of plan, surely, you can't just wander through life aimlessly."

"That's pretty much what you thought I was doing before," Beth said, with a slight irritation to her voice. "At least now I'm happy."

"Which is good, I want you to be happy, but I don't want you to look back and wish you'd done something with your life-"

"Mum!" Lee interrupted, midway through feeding Holly a spoonful of the risotto. "You can't say things like that. Beth *is* doing something with her life. She's got a job she loves, that's a great start."

"That's all well and good, Shirley, but is it a career, though?"

"Maybe," Beth said, shooting her sister a look of gratitude. "Maybe not. I don't know right now. I needed a change, and that is what I did. I'm standing on my own two feet, I'm paying my rent, I'm putting food in the fridge, and that's the last I'm going to say on the subject."

"Well-"

"Mum." Lee's tone was sharper than before, and it had the desired effect; Tina paused, ate a forkful of risotto and let the conversation move on.

Beth breathed a sigh of relief.

In the kitchen, leaving the granddaughter and nearly son-in-law to entertain Tina Davis, Lee and Beth pretended to wash up, while drinking small glasses of wine and sighing about their mother.

"She thinks I'm throwing my life away," Beth said.

"She thought the exact same thing about me, a year and a half ago."

"Yeah, but yours was just a blip on your legendary path to greatness-"

"Beth-"

"No, but seriously, the stakes were higher but she still felt you'd done something. With me, she's convinced I'll never amount to anything. And the thing is, Lee, I don't know what I want to amount to. I don't know what it is that I want to be successful in."

"But you'll figure that out. If you're happy, that's all that matters. You could tell her about your writing…"

"And have her laugh about it? I don't think so - besides, that's just a hobby, it's not something that she's going to think is worthwhile."

"You know she only cares…"

"That's usually my line, when you're ranting!" Beth said, downing the glass of wine. "Don't let me have any more, no matter how much she drives me crazy - I've got to drive back later this evening."

"Sure you don't want to stay the night?" Lee said, but she laughed as she did.

"I think I'll be okay, thanks - anyway, your spare room is taken!"

"Hmmm, I think I need to thank you for that one, don't I?"

Beth laughed and threw a tea towel at her sister.

"Come on, or they'll come looking for us. You dry, I'll wash."

❖ ❖ ❖

By the time she returned home that evening she was drained - not just from the night before, but from trying to be constantly cheerful around her mother who, despite her best intentions, didn't seem to be able to avoid the occasional judgmental comment.

Pouring herself a far larger glass of wine - despite the fact it was a work night - she settled herself into an armchair and dialled Jasmine's number.

It only took three rings for her to answer the phone.

"Beth!" she half-screamed down the phone. "You've been gone forever already!"

Beth laughed; "It's really not been that long. Is work that boring without me?"

"Deathly so. No-one goes out for lunch: apparently the done thing is to eat at your desk and keep working - clearly we weren't in the loop."

"Or we just valued our sanity," Beth said, picturing Jas with a similar sized glass of wine on the other end of the phone.

"Well, mine's gone out the window now that you've gone. They've not even replaced you yet."

"I'm not sure they'll bother," Beth said with a sigh. "I'm not sure they even needed me, to be honest."

She could say it out loud now, now that she had a job she enjoyed and a hobby that made her excited to have free time.

"Anyway, enough about work." Jas, as usual, breezed past the issues to get to what she wanted to discuss. "You've had fireworks, I want the details!"

Beth laughed. "There have definitely been fireworks…"

"I thought you were being picky, but if you've actually found them…"

"So it started in the middle of the ocean," she said, knowing Jas was hanging on every word, and proceeded to tell her every detail of their explosive kiss in the Devon sea.

"Oh. My. God. I can't believe you - you move away and then become exciting?"

"Hey! I've always been exciting!"

"Not kissing gorgeous men, in your underwear, in the middle of the sea, late at night exciting, Beth. Come on, that's a whole other level."

Beth giggled and drank some more wine, enjoying the discussion immensely. "I guess you're right," she said. "It felt pretty damn exciting."

"I bet it did! So, are you meeting him again? Or is he remaining a mysterious stranger…"

"Definitely meeting again. Drinks on Saturday - I'll keep you updated!"

After ten minutes or so of chatting about Jas's boyfriend and their potential future break up, Beth began to yawn and made her apologies.

"I'm exhausted, Jas, sorry - too much of my mother."

"Too much sexual tension with handsome men if you ask me," Jas said. "Fine, but I expect updates next week!"

She promised, and after finishing off the glass she left it by the sink to be washed up tomorrow, along with a few mugs and a plate from the previous couple of days. Bed was just too inviting to consider washing up at eleven at night.

CHAPTER SIXTEEN

By half-five on Saturday, Beth had emptied out nearly every outfit she owned in preparation for her maybe-date that night. She thought she'd settled on an option, but half an hour of throwing clothes around later she had completely rethought it. There was a fine drizzle in the air - lots of complaints about the typical English weather had been bandied around town that morning - and the dress she'd planned to wear didn't seem so appropriate anymore. By half-six, she had finally made a different choice and was in the process of getting dressed, pulling on the white jeans while hopping around to see the clock in the other room.

She swore loudly, realising if she didn't leave in fifteen minutes she was going to be late, and pulled on a black lacy top, before frantically brushing her hair and rummaging through a basket of make-up to find what she was looking for. She didn't even look at the mess she had created in her bedroom - it wasn't worth stressing about, it could be dealt with tomorrow. That was what Sundays were for, after all, weren't they? Clearing up the messes from the rest of the week!

A quick bit of red lippy and a slightly smoky eye, and she felt ready to face the world - and the attractive, mysterious Caspian who made her blood sizzle.

Well, as ready as she was ever going be.

In the end, she was five minutes early; with her hood pulled up high and her coat buttoned up over the outfit that had taken so long to pick, she entered the bar at The Fort, a little inn that was a ten minute walk from her front doorstep, down a little side street of Dartmouth. With a mist hanging in the air, the lights in the window looked particularly inviting, and with one last, reassuring deep breath, she stepped over the threshold.

He was there, even though it was five to seven, sat on a bar stool with his feet solidly on the ground. She watched him for a moment, sat in a dark blue shirt and black jeans, with his collar open. One hand was wrapped around a pint, and the other tapped on the wooden bar beneath it.

There was a man sat next to him, but two spare stools the other side, and so she decided to play along with the charade of meeting by accident; she took the seat on the other side, with the man in between them, and ordered a glass of wine. She felt, rather than saw, his eyes on her, and as the barman poured her a generous glass of rosé, she felt his hand on the small of her back, and heard his voice not far from her ear.

"I'll get this, and the same again for me please," he said, his voice smooth and deep and able to melt Beth right into the seat.

"Fancy meeting you here," Beth said, taking a sip of the slightly-sweet rose, angling her knees a little to face him.

"A coincidence indeed," he said, handing over his card

to pay for the drinks. "You look lovely this evening."

Beth knew she was blushing, but didn't look away. "Thank you," she said. And then the first thing that came into her head popped out - and she couldn't even blame the wine yet for letting words just spill from her mouth with no thought. "You look good with your clothes on too," she said, grinning.

"You've seen me with my clothes on before, but I'll take it as a compliment."

"You should."

"So, Beth. Elizabeth."

"Ah, you remembered the ancient name, Caspian."

"And you remembered mine."

"Hard to forget..." For so many reasons, she thought, taking another sip of her wine as she felt his knee bumping against hers; even through the fabric of both their jeans, she could feel him there.

"You moved to Dartmouth a few weeks ago from..."

"Exeter, so not that far."

"And why Dartmouth?"

"A feeling," she said honestly. "A total feeling of peace when I looked out over the water. It helps that my sister works in Totnes, so I wasn't going completely out of my comfort zone."

"Do you always make such massive decisions based on feelings?"

"How come you get to ask all the questions?" she asked, shooting him a look over her wine glass. "I'll answer that one, but then it's my turn. No, I don't always. It was the first time in a long time I've made a decision based on a strong feeling, and I'm very glad I did."

He nodded, drinking a mouthful of his beer but not asking anything else.

"Where do you live?"

"Strete," he answered. "Just outside of Dartmouth. Although I'm away for work quite a lot of the time."

"What do you do?"

"How many questions do you get?"

"More than this."

"I'm a publicist," he said. "Mainly for publishers, but a few other clients as well."

"Where do you go away to?"

"London, Birmingham, occasionally Edinburgh, every now and then New York... I do a lot of my work over the internet, but sometimes it's just got to be me in person." His knee brushed against hers once more, and she couldn't resist pressing hers back into his a little more firmly.

"A powerful man - what makes you live down here the rest of the time then?"

"Honestly? My mum."

Beth took that in for a minute, taking another drink

from her glass before realising that, without having eaten dinner that evening, the wine was definitely going straight to her head.

"My relationship with my mum isn't quite as close as that," she admitted. "I don't think I would cope well with her round the corner."

"No?"

"Oh I love her, don't get me wrong, but she can be very... judgy. She was down here this week, in fact, and as much as she tried to keep it pleasant, she couldn't help but tell me all the mistakes I was making with my life."

"You don't look like you've made a mistake to me."

"I don't feel like I've made a mistake. I've been more happy in the six weeks or so that I've been here than I have been in years."

He raised his glass to her, and she lifted hers to tap against it. "Sounds like you're winning to me."

"I thought you were the winner," she said with a grin, thinking back to that brief kiss he had taken as his prize.

"I'm not sure I'm as happy as you are." He paused, and finished the beer in front of him. "I'm sorry, I don't normally share quite so freely." Their knees had been pressed together for so long now that it felt natural, and Beth couldn't resist trailing her fingers across the black fabric covering his knee, just for a moment, as she spoke.

"I don't either," she said. "I blame the wine."

"I never drink this quickly. I think you make me nervous." He spoke as he looked her directly in the eye, and at that moment it was as if there was no-one else in the room but them, and the energy that crackled between them - the fireworks that were building, that she needed to feel explode before too long. One good kiss just wasn't enough.

"You make me forget to think through what I'm saying - although perhaps I've never been great at keeping my foot out of my mouth."

He reached out, his warm hand against her cheek, his thumb grazing her lips, and she closed her eyes for a moment to simply feel the sensations that were flooding through her.

It was a heady feeling that took her breath away, and when he pressed his lips against hers for the third time that week, hers responded immediately. He, at least, seemed aware of their location, and pulled away gently before she quite reached his short dark hair that she was desperate to bury her fingers in.

He didn't take his hand away from her cheek for a few moments, and she felt her head spin.

"I need to eat," she finally said. "Sorry, it's not subtle, but I've not eaten since breakfast and that wine has gone straight to my head."

"And here I was thinking it was an amazing kiss making your head spin," Cas said with a smile as he motioned to the barman and signalled for two menus.

"Oh, I think that has a lot to do with it," she said, and his grin grew broader. "Don't go getting arrogant though."

"Oh, this is not one sided, Beth. Kissing you is a whole other experience…"

"You feel the fireworks too?" She couldn't believe the words were really coming out of her mouth - was she really asking this fine figure in front of her for confirmation that the kiss had been incredible? Blame the wine, blame the kiss - she needed to know.

"Catherine wheels, rockets, Roman candles - you name them, they're there when we kiss."

She glanced at the menu, choosing fish and chips because it was the first thing she saw, then looked straight back at him. "You are a mysterious man, you know that?"

"Not with you, I just blurt everything out."

"You're grumpy one minute, charming the next, brutally honest and then I feel there's things about you I know absolutely nothing about. A complete enigma."

"Makes it more exciting doesn't it?"

Beth closed one eye and regarded him. "Maybe. One more question: how the hell do you get home from the beach?"

CHAPTER SEVENTEEN

"I run. I run there, swim for an hour, and run back."

"Every night?" She was a little incredulous.

"Every night that I'm here, yeah."

"That's dedication. Why?"

"Why not?"

"I can think of lots of reasons," Beth said, reaching for cutlery as their two fish and chips were delivered to the bar. "Sleep, watching television, eating chocolate…"

"I can still do all those things," he said, tucking in. "Kissing pretty girls in the ocean - it's not all bad."

"I'm going to hope I'm the first person you've nearly scared to death out there and then ended up making a move on."

"Wouldn't you like to know," he said, a glint in his eye that made Beth laugh.

"Seriously though, why?"

"I don't really talk about it," he said, filling his mouth with chips in a bid to avoid talking.

"But you just said you end up telling me things without even thinking about it."

"Very true. Are you sure you want to know? It's not exactly first-date material."

"We spent ten minutes talking about how explosive our kiss was. I'm not sure we need to worry about the traditional rules of a date." Inside there was definitely part of her - a part that she was a little embarrassed by - that was excited by the fact that he considered it a proper date.

"Okay. Well, I had a cancer scare, about five years ago. I was a little overweight, ate rubbish, didn't exercise and thought I was a gonner. Decided then and there to make a massive change, and the exercise is what lets me still eat the chocolate, and the fish and chips, every now and again."

Beth digested that for a moment. "I certainly get the need to make a change, but I'm not sure I'd have that dedication."

"It's a routine. Once you're into it, it stops being effort after a while. And swimming in the ocean at night has got a certain charm, don't you think?"

"Definitely. It's wonderfully free, I'll give you that. And then, of course, it depends who you meet when you decide to go for a reckless, spontaneous swim."

"Well, I'm just learning of those benefits."

Dinner made Beth's head feel slightly less woozy, and as the conversation flowed easily - with the help of another glass of wine - she felt like she at least had an image of who Caspian really was. The time seemed to disappear, and before they knew it the inn was closing and they were forced out into the rain, taking shelter in the doorway as they said their goodbyes.

"Maybe we could do this again, a little less spontaneously," Beth said, the wine making her brave, the proximity to Caspian making her reckless.

"I'm away all week," he said, "Up in London for work. How about next Sunday evening?"

"Sounds like a good plan," Beth said. "Although you can't keep me up too late, it is a work night, after all."

"You make me sound like a very corrupting influence," Caspian said.

"I think you might be."

He didn't need to hear that twice. The doorway was dark and small and he moved closer to Beth so that her back was against the red brick wall. His hands settled on either side of his head, fingers in her hair, and his lips just millimetres away from her mouth, as he murmured, "I think you might be the one corrupting me."

There were no more words, then, and no soft kisses; this was pure passion, as tongues met and stubble grazed against cheek, fireworks exploded that threatened to make Beth forget every sensible thing she had ever thought. His body was solid against hers, the wall cold against her back, and she felt like that pressure was the only thing keeping her upright. That and her arms that were wrapped around his neck, with her fingers exploring the hair at the nape it. His legs, his chest, everything he had was pressed against her petite body, making the air leave her lungs and the wine and passion swirl through her head like a mist.

And then they pulled away, hearing a car drive past, and he rested his forehead against hers as their breath mingled, equally ragged.

"Fireworks," she whispered, and he laughed.

"Fireworks."

"I'll walk you home," he offered, once words were at his command again, and she smiled and accepted the offer, despite the rain and the short distance, knowing that spending more time with him was something she definitely wanted.

"How are you getting home?" she asked, as they strolled together, her arm brushing his, her steps in time with his.

"I drove in... but I think you made me forget that, and I've had too many beers to drive it back. I guess I'll run."

"Run? But it's gone eleven, Caspian, and it's raining."

"Taxis aren't very common round here, although I guess I could give it a go."

They reached her doorstep, and she toyed with an idea

that could ruin everything. And then she just blurted it out.

"You can stay the night here, if you want. On the sofa," she said hurriedly, not wanting him to get an impression of her that would put him off, or make him think she was easy - although the image of him in her bed, that torso beneath her sheets, was certainly one she would happily ruminate on later.

"You don't have to do that," he said, pausing in the doorway to the fish and chip shop. "You live in a chip shop?"

"Above it, idiot," she said with a laugh. "And I want to; I'll worry about you running home, and you're right, taxis are like gold dust round here. I'm sure the sofa's very comfortable, although I've never tested it."

He smiled; "Okay then. Lead the way."

Beth went through the complicated process of opening the shop door, resetting their alarm and then unlocking her own front door - something which had apparently put off people who were previously interested, but didn't bother Beth. She remembered, at the last minute, the mess in which she had left her flat, and she hoped she had confined it all to her bedroom where she could close the door and pretend she wasn't a chaotic person.

As they slipped through the door, she quickly closed her bedroom door and glanced around the living room, feeling like it was an acceptable level of tidy for a drunken sleepover.

"Do want another drink?" Beth asked, suddenly feeling a little shy.

"Well, since I'm not driving, thanks."

"I've only got wine."

"That'll do!" He wandered over to the window and glanced out at the dark vista, where lights on the other side of the water could just be seen through the drizzle and mist. "I thought it was a bit weird, living above a chip shop without your own entrance," he said.

"Charming," Beth muttered under her breath, none too quietly.

"But I can see why now. This view, it's fantastic!"

"Well, you can see why I fell for it - it's even better in daylight." She passed him a large glass of white wine.

"I bet it is."

They sat down together on the sofa, a little space between them, and for a few moments no words were spoken.

"I had a great evening," Beth said, with a slightly shy smile playing on her lips, when the silence got too much for her.

"So did I."

They fell into chatting about their jobs, and after downing the dregs of her wine she admitted to him that in her spare time, she'd started a novel.

"Wow. How's it going?"

"Really good, actually. I've never done anything like this before, but the words just seem to flow when I sit down with a pen and paper so I thought, while they're coming, I might as well write them down!"

"You should definitely carry on with it. So many people talk about writing a novel, but few people actually manage to do it."

She smiled, pleased he hadn't just laughed her comment off or made fun of it. Stifling a yawn, she glanced at the clock, and was shocked to see it was already one in the morning.

"I think I should go to bed," she said, "Because if I have any more wine I may just pass out right here."

He finished his glass. "Probably a sensible suggestion. Thank you, again, for the sofa; I actually, for once, did not feel like running."

"Let me go and find you a blanket and a pillow." She disappeared off into her bedroom, which was every bit as messy as she'd remembered it being, and took a moment to heap all the clothes she had tried on and then discarded everywhere onto a chair in the corner of the room, rather than on her bed or the floor. She rummaged in a drawer to find a blanket, and then took two pillows from her own bed, as she knew she didn't have any spare. Having lived alone in a one-bedroom flat for a long time meant she didn't exactly plan for overnight visitors.

When she came back out, he had washed up the glasses, and was using a blue stripy tea-towel to dry and polish them.

"You didn't need to do that."

"Least I could do," he said, as she lay the pillow and blanket down on the sofa.

"I'll see you in the morning then?" he said, walking towards her, drying his hands on his jeans.

"Don't disappear before I wake up," she said, taking a step forward herself and feeling the warmth of his breath in the air in front of her.

"I'm not Cinderella."

"Goodnight, then."

"Goodnight." He leant forward as she had hoped he would, and she stood on tiptoes to reach him faster. Just like before, when their lips met sparks flew, and Beth tangled her fingers in that short dark hair like she had imagined, and let him kiss her until her head felt dizzy and her legs felt weak.

It was she who broke it off this time, placing a hand against his chest and feeling his heart hammering beneath it, just as she was sure hers was. "If we carry on like that, I'll never make it into that bedroom," she said, with a sad smile, knowing how close she was to breaking her no sex on the first date rule.

"Is it awful if that just makes me want to kiss you more?"

She shook her head. "No, but I'm drunk, and you're drunk, and as a rule I don't have men stay over on a first date."

"So I'm the exception."

"You are most definitely an exception," she said, pressing her lips to his once more and then disentangling herself from him. "But I don't think I should sleep with you when we're both drunk." She couldn't say the words in her head, even now, even when she felt the room spinning; that this felt so explosive, she wanted to do it properly. If - and she had no idea if this would be the case - if this was going to be more than just going out one night, or making out in the middle of the sea, she wanted to remember ever minute. Not fall into bed drunk with him because he made her feel so deliciously on fire...

"Goodnight, Beth."

"Goodnight, Caspian," she said, and she walked away, feeling like closing that bedroom door was the hardest thing she'd ever done.

Despite the wine and the pent up energy, Beth found she did sleep well that night, although her dreams took on a life of their own, playing out scenes that she had closed the door on the night before. When she woke at seven the next morning, hot and bothered and her mouth dry with thirst, it took her a moment or two to remember why her room was in such a state, and that there was well over six foot of gorgeous man asleep on her sofa, on the other side of that white wooden door.

Slipping on a nightie - since she'd apparently gone to sleep in her underwear - she quietly opened the door and headed to the kitchen. She paused at the sofa, checking to make sure he really was still there, and couldn't help but linger when she realised he was sleeping in just his boxers, and had thrown the blanket off. It was his legs that got her; long, tanned and muscled, curled up on her small white sofa, covered in a fine layer of dark hair.

She tore her eyes away, knowing she shouldn't stare at him when he was asleep, then padded to the kitchen and tried to be as quiet as she could getting a glass of water. Next stop was the bathroom, where she brushed her teeth and looked horrified at the state of her appearance in the mirror, make-up smudged where she had not bothered to remove it the night before. The shower, she thought, would be too loud at this time in the morning when Caspian still looked so peacefully asleep, so she made do with giving her face a good scrub and moisturise, until she at least felt a little more human. Then a brush of her hair, and she looked as though she would like to look when she had just woken up in the morning - fresh as a daisy.

It was an illusion, but one she wasn't planning to break with the handsome man that she had not even slept with yet.

When she re-entered the living room, Caspian was sat up, the blanket over his lap, still topless and watching her walk back in.

"Sorry, I didn't mean to wake you up."

"I struggle to sleep past seven, even when I'm in my own bed."

She put the kettle on, wanting a cup of tea to get her morning started. "Was the sofa all right?"

"Slept like a baby," he answered, stretching out his arms. "And surprisingly not too hungover this morning."

"I'm shattered, but no, not too bad either. Tea?"

"Coffee, please, if you've got it."

She rummaged in the cupboard for the emergency stash she kept for if Lee came round, and set to making them both hot drinks, pleased she had bought milk and bread the day before so she could at least offer something for breakfast. Now she was working regularly, paying the rent and food bills wasn't so much of a stress - but it didn't mean she was always the most organised when it came to filling the fridge.

She had just finished pouring the boiling water when she felt a hand on the small of her back, and when she turned he was there, making her crane her neck a little to look right into his eyes.

"I don't think I can wait until next Sunday to kiss you again," he said, and inside her she felt a fluttering of nerves and excitement at the gorgeous, sexy words spilling from his mouth.

"You don't have to," she whispered back, putting down the teaspoon and closing the gap between them.

Somewhere in the time since she'd spied him asleep on the sofa, he'd slipped his jeans back on, although they weren't buttoned and his shirt was still very much on the floor. She was aware of the feel of his bare skin against her, the fact that she wore only a thin nightie over her underwear, and that his stubble was scratching deliciously against her skin as he pressed his lips first to the side of her neck, then beneath her earlobe, then tantalisingly close to her lips, making a quiet moan escape from them.

Then there was no messing; their lips met, her back pressed into the sink, teas and coffees forgotten in this moment of pure heat. She didn't care this time that she was out of breath, didn't care that there was no possible way she could stop this train of events. He was so warm and solid beneath her hands, and made her feel so electrified, and if you couldn't bend the rules in times like that, when could you?

Besides, she liked being spontaneous.

Once again it was her who broke the kiss, and she revelled in the look of desire in his eyes for a moment, feeling in that moment like the most powerful, luckiest woman in the world, before crossing her arms and pulling the nightie over her head, dropping it into a heap on the floor.

After all, he'd seen her in her underwear before; kissed her in her underwear before.

"My room's a mess," she said, and he shrugged.

"I don't care. But we don't have to-"

"I want to. I'm not drunk anymore, Caspian - except on those kisses."

She led him to that door that had been so hard to close the previous night and pushed it open, not caring about the pile of clothes in the corner or the fact that they'd technically only had one date. This was another day, it could count as two; and to be honest, she didn't know if she had ever in her life felt a connection like the one they seemed to share.

His unbuttoned jeans came off easily, and, feeling like every touch of his fingertips on her bare skin was burning a trail of the fireworks to come, Beth kicked the door closed.

CHAPTER EIGHTEEN

If she had slept well the night before, it was nothing to how she slept that morning, her legs tangled with Caspian's beneath the white duvet cover, hair thoroughly mussed and energy spent - at least for now. They had both slipped into a deep, sated sleep that lasted well through the morning, their hot drinks forgotten, cold on the side, the possibility of breakfast a distant memory.

Caspian awoke first, but didn't move; Beth's blonde hair was spread over his arm, her legs entwined with his, her back pressed against him, and for a few minutes he watched her sleeping, feeling a little in shock at how this week had played out. When he'd seen her there, on the beach in her dripping wet underwear, he'd known there'd been a spark; known he wanted her - but he hadn't realised how overwhelming that feeling would become, nor how passionate he could have found simply kissing her. And this morning, well... there weren't words for how perfect the morning had been, even down to this, holding her and watching her breathe slowly in and out, shafts of sunlight making her hair glow golden on the white pillowcase.

Beth rolled over then, and slowly blinked, her eyes adjusting to the sunlight from the unclosed curtains, and beamed when she saw him propped up on an arm next to her.

"Good morning,"

"Good morning, again."

"I feel like I've slept forever," she said, yawning and stretching her legs beneath the covers, although they reached nowhere near the end of the bed.

Cas glanced at his watch. "It's not far off twelve, so we've slept for a while."

"I was exhausted, apparently."

His eyes glinted as he grinned. "I can't think why."

She laughed, a deep throaty laugh that shook her whole body, and his as well, entwined as they still were.

"I think there's a few reasons," she said. "But I am absolutely starving, and you distracted me this morning from tea and breakfast."

He leant and pressed a kiss to her lips. "A bad distraction?"

She shook her head. "A delicious distraction."

"Good. So, that date next Sunday - we're still on?"

"I'm in."

He grinned. "I'll pick you up at six, is that okay? Since I did promise to have you home at a reasonable time, for a work night."

Beth was fairly sure the chances of her getting an early night, if the morning's activities were anything to go by, were rather slim, but a six o'clock date sounded perfect.

"Do you want lunch?" Beth asked, sitting up but keeping the duvet clutched to her chest.

"I'm afraid I've got to dash off," he said, reaching out of the bed to grab his clothes. "Sorry."

"It's okay," she said, but she was sure the disappointment showed on her face. She knew she was being greedy; she'd had all night, all morning, all of him…

"I take my mum out for lunch on a Sunday," he explained, pulling on his jeans and searching for his shirt, before realising it was still in the living room. "Whenever I'm here."

"That's nice," she said, waiting until his back was turned to reach out and find her own underwear - although her nightie, she knew, was still in a pool on the kitchen floor.

She hesitated to get out of the bed, until Caspian offered her his hand. "I've seen you in your underwear before," he said, and though the comment caused her cheeks to glow red, she shed the duvet and followed him into the living room so they could retrieve their respective clothing items.

"Let me get properly dressed," she said, "and I'll walk you out."

He was fully clothed when she reappeared in a simple dress, having dragged a brush through her hair once more that morning, and even though his shirt was a little creased, he still looked as good as he had done the night before.

"Thanks for a lovely evening, and morning, Beth," he said.

"You're very welcome, Caspian." She paused. "I know how awful this sounds, but I feel like I should probably know your last name..."

"Oh, god, yes, definitely. Caspian Blackwell." He reached out his hand to shake hers, and she giggled at the formality.

"Beth Davis."

"Elizabeth..."

"Just because I use your full name..."

"Yours is beautiful."

She screwed her face up. "You're just flattering me."

"Never," he said.

Beth led the way down the stairs, where the chip shop was bustling with lunch time trade. She saw Sam catch her eyes, saw him clock Caspian, but she said nothing, not even a greeting.

She was pretty sure she heard a wolf whistle as they exited the front of the shop, and resolved to kill him later - or at least glare at him a lot.

"I'm very glad I saved you from drowning," he said as they stood on the side of the street, the water calm in the sunshine that had reappeared from wherever it had been hiding.

"I'm glad I accidentally left my bra in your towel," Beth answered, her tongue wetting her lips in anticipation of the kiss that she was sure was coming. Several kisses down, and her whole body still hummed at his presence, craved that contact, that reaction that he caused to ignite within her.

They kissed without caring that people were passing them in the street, nor that they were in the way, and then he was gone, and Beth couldn't help but watch him as he disappeared round the corner to wherever he had left his car the night before.

She wasn't surprised that there was a comment when she returned to the shop; Sam couldn't resist, even with several baskets of chips on the go and a shop full of customers.

"Quick work, Beth!"

"How do you know he's not my husband, or some long-distance boyfriend?" she asked, sticking her tongue out when she thought no-one else was looking.

"Pretty sure I recognise him from round here," he said with a laugh.

Beth rolled her eyes, but laughed too; he could tease all he liked, but it wasn't going to stop her feeling like she was floating from the last twenty-four hours of bliss.

After a slice of toast or two to settle her slightly

hungover stomach and stop her feeling so ravenous, Beth finally climbed in the shower and spent far too long enjoying the feeling of the water pouring over her and grinning to herself. She couldn't help but replay the night - and the morning - in her head, marvelling at how things had changed since she'd made the decision to move to Dartmouth and press reset on her life.

A very welcome text from Lee was waiting for her when she finally got out of the shower, feeling a little dizzy from the heat and the steam, and threw herself onto her unmade bed.

Having a Sunday dinner at 4ish, fancy joining us? Sorry for the late notice, I forget how close you are! L xx

She replied as soon as she'd read it. *Sounds perfect, I'm starving and have gossip!!! Xx*

Intriguing! X

Well, there was no way Lee wasn't going to ask with a tease like that, Beth thought, but she didn't care - she was ready to tell her big sister about this man that had appeared in her life when he was least expected, and who was as keen to try being spontaneous as she was.

With no mad rush to get there, Beth took her time blow drying her hair, picking out another set of matching underwear - pink, this time - and another shift dress that was so simple to wear when the weather was this pleasant. She considered tidying up, but decided that could be done another day; even with work, it wasn't like she didn't have the time, and besides, she felt like the week before their planned date might drag a little. Belatedly she had realised that she didn't even have his phone number, nor he hers, and while she tried stalking him on social media for a good half an hour while she procrastinated about getting dressed, she could find no trace of him.

The only mention she did find online was a simple website for his publicist business, although regrettably there was no photograph. (She thought about mentioning that to him when she next saw him - after all, he was bound to be exceedingly photogenic and she felt as though it might persuade people they needed his service - but then realised how stalkerish that might look.)It did have a contact number, although she didn't think she'd dare ring his work number unless she had no choice, but at least it was something. It was too easy to think he was all a figment of her imagination without anything tangible of him to call or check.

At least she had his surname - although she guessed there weren't that many Caspians living in the South West of England.

With an hour before she needed to be at Lee's, Beth positioned herself in front of that view, with the sunlight glinting off the windows and the water, and lost herself in writing once more, remembering Caspian's words of encouragement with a glow.

"When you said you were cooking a roast dinner, I presumed you actually meant James," Beth said, sat at her sister's dining room table, watching a slightly flustered looking Lee balance two plates while trying not to knock the gravy off.

"Shut up, you, I can cook!"

"I know you *can*, but you don't tend to choose to. And you're sure I can't help?" Holly was happily playing with toys in her high chair, and James was showering after finishing his shift - and yet Lee had insisted she was fine.

"No, no, I can do this..."

"Just because you're soon to be married again, doesn't mean you have to present the perfect image of domesticity, you know," Beth said, grabbing a dish of carrots that had narrowly missed being knocked all over the floor. "You're a modern woman, there's nothing wrong with letting James cook."

She could tell her sister was getting wound up, but found teasing her to still be amusing.

"I know that," Lee said through gritted teeth. "But he always cooks, and I want to do this."

"Mama!" Holly called, seemingly for no other reason that to get attention, and Lee paused to fuss over her before getting back to dishing up.

"You can get the cutlery out, if you want to help. And cut the smart comments!"

"Yes ma'am," Beth said with a giggle, setting the table and with a smile plastered on her face.

"And once we're done with dinner, I want to know why you can't stop smiling, and what the gossip is, all right?"

"Okay," Beth said. "But I warn you, it may not be suitable for little ears - or male ones for that matter!"

They were both cracking up with laughter when James walked in wearing a t-shirt and jeans, rather than his uniform, and with damp hair that had clearly been freshly towel dried. "Do I want to know?" he asked with a grin, and they both shook their heads.

Despite her teasing, the roast was delicious, and Beth and James made sure to repeatedly praise the chef; Holly ended up with gravy in her hair, which they assumed meant she'd enjoyed it.

"I'll wash up," he said, as Beth tried to clear the table. "Go on, you two go and sit in the other room."

"Thanks love," Lee said, leaning over carefully to give him a quick kiss with a filthy Holly in her arms. "Let me go and clean this monster up, Beth, then we can catch up, okay?"

"I'll make the tea!"

"There's wine if you want it," James offered, "We can always drop you back."

"No, thanks - had plenty last night, think tea is all I want today!"

"Fair enough."

Lee reappeared as Beth was carrying two mugs into the living room, and once Holly was settled on the carpet with a toy, she turned all her attention to her little sister - in size as well as age - and readied herself for the gossip.

"Spill, then, you've had me intrigued all day!"

"I like to be of interest," she said with a smile, feeling

her cheeks warming a little.

"Who is he then?!"

"Who said there was a 'he' involved?"

"I can just tell!"

Beth laughed. "Okay, okay, it's a he. We met at the beach, swimming."

"Very romantic," Lee said, sipping her tea and waiting for more.

Beth wasn't sure whether it had been romantic or just downright sensual, but she didn't contradict.

"So, I need no judgment now-"

"No judgment here," Lee said, holding up a hand in the air. "Not your mother!"

"Oh, and no mentioning it to her, either. Anyway, so it was a moonlit swim in the sea-"

"Not very safe, Beth."

"Sounds like judgment to me!"

Lee put a finger to her lips and said no more.

"And I had spontaneously decided to swim in my underwear." Lee gasped. "And when I got out, he lent me a towel, and-"

"You did not have sex with him on the beach?!"

"No, I didn't, as a matter of fact, Miss Non-Judgmental. But he did end up with my bra in his possession - completely innocently, I might add - and that was that."

"So nothing happened?" Lee asked, moving to the edge of the sofa to hear better.

"Not that night..."

Lee grinned and waited.

"So then I see him at work, with his mother, and of course he mentions the underwear and that he could return it to me when he swims that night... And one thing led to another-"

"You can't skip details like that!" Lee protested.

"I can! You're my sister, you don't get all the details. So, there was some pretty amazing kissing in the ocean, I'll tell you that - and then last night we went out on a date."

"A proper date?"

"Yep, dinner, drinks..."

"And...?"

Beth knew she was blushing now. "It was amazing, Lee. He is drop dead gorgeous, I mean, you couldn't make up how tall, dark and handsome he is - and he stayed over. On the sofa."

Lee's face dropped at the end. "Oh, I thought..."

"Well, it was only the first date," Beth said, but she was smiling. "What happened this morning is a whole other matter..."

"So, that's why you can't stop smiling!" Lee said, grinning herself. "And you're seeing him again?"

Beth nodded. "Sunday. I don't know what will happen,

but I'm okay with just going with the flow, to be honest. I wasn't looking for a man..."

"That's when they come along," Lee said. "When you least expect it - and with the worst possible timing, in my case!"

"Hey," Beth said, sipping her rapidly cooling tea. "It all worked out in the end, didn't it?"

"It did," Lee said. "Although I still think mum thinks I've lost my mind, getting remarried, starting a family so soon after getting divorced."

"She adores Holly, you know that. And she's the queen of judging, that's not going to change overnight I'm afraid to say. Besides, all the timing proves is that Nathan - scumbag that he was - was not the right person for you. He wasn't your happily ever after."

"I suppose you're right. And is mystery man your happily ever after?"

"Lee, I don't even know if I believe in happily ever afters for myself. I'm happy right now - I'm good with that."

Lee gave her knee a squeeze. "It might be him, it might not, but you're young, Beth - there is definitely the perfect match out there for you."

"Easy to say when you've found yours!"

CHAPTER NINETEEN

As predicted, the week dragged for Beth, even doing a job she loved. For two evenings in a row she sat with her notebook on her lap, not writing, daydreaming and struggling to focus. It was by the third night that she'd had a serious chat with herself: this was not the way she was willing to spend her life. She was not going to wile her life away waiting for a date with a mysterious man. She was not going to stop doing the things she loved because there was a man in her life. She was Beth Davis, she had moved her life, she had started again, and as dreamy as Caspian was, he was not the centre of the universe.

She needed to be the centre of her own universe.

And so on Wednesday night, with a cup of tea and pen, she let the words flow out of her once more, taking inspiration from the grounds at Greenway, and wrote a scene that made her want to cry - first with sadness, then with pride at the emotion she felt she was evoking - in herself, at least. Whether anyone else would feel that way was another question.

Adelaide sat on the wrought-iron bench, watching a

mother push a perambulator past the lake, seemingly trying to get the baby within to sleep. Her heart hurt; she was sure that was all lost to her now. The hopes she had harboured all her life of a love-match, of children, of a life in the country where she could enjoy days out in the park...gone. Tears wended their way down her cheeks. Yes, her sleuthing had solved the murder. Yes, for the first time in months, she felt safe to be outside, not worrying that the murderer was bent on killing off another member of the family.

But now she knew. Knew her husband to be a murderer. Knew that he had killed his father to be able to get a divorce. Would she have been next? He had sworn not, when he'd begged her not to go to the police...

There was no hope of falling in love with her husband now. And no hope of anyone else ever wanting to marry the divorced wife of a convicted murderer.

She lost herself in the words, even re-reading everything she had written so far in this beautiful notebook and feeling like there was a real story in there. Sure, it was rough, and it needed polishing, but she had never produced anything in her life that she had felt so proud of. She wasn't sure she'd ever created anything, not of her own volition.

She threw herself into tidying and organising her flat that weekend, realising that, somewhere along the way, there were boxes she had forgotten to unpack and dishes that had ended up stacked and waiting to be washed. She wished she were one of those people who washed up as soon as a meal was finished - or even while it was being cooked; one of those people who put clothes away as soon as they were dry, and never ended up with a pile of clothes on a chair or in a basket. But try as she might, she just was not one of those people, and so her adult life had been spent leaving chores she really should complete and then catching up on them at weekends. Of course, when her weekends had been more filled with late nights and hangovers, there was even less motivation to get it done.

Now, when there was something to look forward to on Sunday evening, she found that motivation - and by lunch time on Sunday, the flat looked better than when she moved in.

Sunday roast at 6pm, James is cooking, you're very welcome! X

Beth grinned; her sister was, as always, trying to look after her. She was fairly sure Lee thought she was living off fish and chips, which was only half true. Granted, a fish and chip shop being below was a dangerous temptation, and there had already been another evening that week where Sam had begged her to step in and had paid her in cash and a fish supper. But she was making meals in between, and as nice as roast dinner sounded, tonight was already spoken for.

Thank you, but got plans already, remember! ;) x

Ah yes, the hot date?! The reply came almost instantly.

We'll see!!

Just a smiley face was sent back, and Beth grinned. She felt a bubbling in her stomach that she was sure was nerves, but also a hint of excitement. She was finding it hard to believe that the date last week, that night, that morning, had been as amazing as she remembered. But when she did remember it... sure, she was nervous, but there was definitely anticipation mixed in there too.

She began getting ready early, remembering last week's indecision, starting with a relaxing hot shower - well, a shower that was meant to be relaxing, but ended up with her cutting her leg on a razor blade that was clearly past its best and hopping round the bathroom, trying to get a plaster before she bled over her nice white towels.

"Perfect," she muttered to herself, sat on the bed with her hair wrapped up in one towel and another around her, feeling cross and irritated and not the relaxed, sexy Beth she had hoped to be when she emerged from the shower.

She let herself glance out towards the water, not worrying too much about people seeing her in just her towel, and took a few deep, calming breaths as she watched the sun glistening off the water, and the boats moving gently with the motion of the water. In, out. In, out. This was going to be a good evening, she could feel it, and a couple of cuts on her legs were not going to ruin that.

She considered waiting outside but thought this might look a little desperate. While she was keen to see Caspian again, it wasn't just desperation that made her consider it. She was trying to spare him having to come in and talk to Sam, who would undoubtedly be working in the fish shop that evening. There was an external buzzer to her door; perhaps he would figure that out.

She had no idea where they were going on this date. She presumed it would include dinner, but at the moment she couldn't think of food; her stomach was full of flutters and jitters.

At exactly six that evening there was a knock on her door. She smiled: he had obviously got past the security and up to knock directly. She had one last glance in the mirror - black jeans, black pumps and a floaty blue top, that she hoped would be appropriate wherever they went - grabbed a handbag and opened the door.

There he was.

She'd wondered in the intervening week whether he could possibly be as good looking as she'd remembered, but oh my, he was. He was dressed in black jeans himself, with a dark grey shirt that was open at the collar; his black hair was slightly ruffled as if he'd run his hands through it recently and his skin looked a gorgeous brown where he had clearly been enjoying the sun. She wondered whether he swam in sunlight as well as in moonlight, for that would explain the gorgeous colour he was.

"Hi," she said with a smile, and his white teeth were on full display as he grinned back.

"Evening," he said. "Shall we?"

Beth nodded, locking the door behind her and heading down the steps. Sam was swapping over with a new recruit for the evening and made no comment out loud - although Beth was sure she'd hear something about this later. They stepped outside into the warm balmy evening air and Beth glanced at Caspian questioningly. "Lead the way," she said.

And he did.

Without a word he grabbed her hand and pulled her across the road. She knew she was paying no attention to whether there was any traffic, but simply trusting him to move her safely across. In her mind, all the thoughts were about the fact that he had taken her hand. The thrill of feeling his warm, slightly rough hand around hers; the tingle from where they connected; that silly teenage feeling when someone touches you when you're not quite expecting it.

"The ferry?" she said, raising her eyebrows as they stood in line by the wall where she waited every workday.

"You'll see," he said with a grin.

"Well, this is just like my morning commute," she said with a laugh.

"Lucky you," he said. "I think some people would kill for a commute like this; when they're stuck in their cars queuing to get into London."

"Believe me, I'm not complaining. So, how's your week been?" she asked.

"Busy," he said. "I had meetings in London so was up there for four days. Got back late last night, took Mum out for lunch today and now - here I am!"

"You're a very busy man," she said. "Maybe I'm lucky you made room in your schedule for me!"

Caspian shook his head; "I would have rearranged the

schedule, if it hadn't worked," he said. "I've been looking forward to this evening."

"Me too," Beth said honestly, well aware that he had not let go of her hand, even though he was no longer propelling her forward. There was a moment where their eyes met; where tension crackled in the air; when she was reminded of last Sunday morning, of the possibilities that lay ahead of them. It was almost overwhelming and so she couldn't help but make a joke just to lighten the tension a little - as delicious as it was to revel in it.

"It'll be even more exciting when I know what we're actually doing. I hope it's not rock climbing or white water rafting," she said with a laugh. "I know what you're like with your sports and I'm definitely not dressed for that."

He laughed. "You look beautiful," he said, not shy about complimenting her although she couldn't help but look away at the words. "But no, don't worry, no extreme sports - not today, anyway. Maybe for the next date." He winked and she laughed as the ferry came into port and they boarded, along with eight or so cars and a few foot passengers.

Instead of taking the smaller ferry that she usually caught straight to Greenway, they had boarded the main ferry between Dartmouth and Kingswear, and were soon standing and looking over the side as the boat cut through the water beneath them. It was still warm, and Beth kept her sunglasses on as she looked over the water, back at her home.

"Beautiful view, isn't it," she said, feeling Caspian's fingertips against hers and finding it hard to think of anything to talk about that wasn't the weather, or the setting.

"Mmhmm," he agreed, glancing down at her and then back towards Dartmouth. "I've always loved getting this ferry. We used to take the car on and even then my mum would insist on us all getting out and standing here - no matter the weather, or how short the journey was!"

Beth laughed; "She sounds like my sort of woman. Appreciate what's on your doorstep!"

The journey was slow, but neither minded; the sun glinted off the water and reflected in their smiles, their laughter carrying across the fairly calm waters surrounding them.

They disembarked into Kingswear, and walked up the hill still hand-in-hand.

"Do you miss it down here, when you're working away?" Beth asked.

"Definitely - especially the sea. Although when I'm here, sometimes I find myself missing the bustle of the city... the chance of getting a taxi without booking a week in advance. The anonymity of stepping into a street where no-one knew you at primary school or chats with your great aunt on a regular basis."

"Anonymity is overrated," Beth said. "It's all well and good until you actually need someone around..."

"You've got a point," he agreed, pulling her sideways into a yellow building.

"Where on Earth are we going, Caspian?"

"I promise we're staying on Earth, Elizabeth," he said

with a grin, giving nothing away. Beth glanced around at the signs and notices on the walls.

"A train station?"

"Excellent deduction, Miss Marple."

"To where?"

"Do you ever just throw yourself in the moment and not ask questions?" he asked with a grin, and she opened her mouth to respond again, before shutting it and following his advice.

He already had tickets, it seemed, and they passed through a gate onto a platform where a regal looking steam train stood. It felt like something from the movies, or like a grand visit to the past; a relic of a romantic time long gone where train journeys were new and a great adventure, and where people ran along platforms waving goodbye or declaring their love. She almost voiced her thoughts before realising that they sounded like she spent a little too much of her time watching old romantic films - or that she was expecting some declaration of love herself, which she most definitely wasn't.

"You can talk you know," Caspian said, raising his eyebrows at her prolonged silence.

"Well, I wasn't sure if I'd get into trouble," she said, sticking her tongue out for good effect.

"I think you're all sorts of trouble," Caspian said. "Come on."

"Where?"

"All aboard!" he said with childish glee, pulling her

down the platform to an open door labelled 'Carriage C'.

"Good evening sir, madam." At the door was a man dressed in a green uniform, with a black hat and shiny black buttons. "May I see your tickets please?"

Caspian handed them over, and the gentleman clipped both before handing them back. "Please follow me."

Beth didn't speak - not because she was afraid of getting in trouble, but because she was a little in awe of her surroundings. Green lamps lit the walls, although the sun still streamed in from outside. In the middle of the carriage was a chandelier, which felt like it belonged in a fancy dining room rather than a train, and gave the whole place a delicious air of decadence and intrigue. The tables were set, almost exclusively for two, with white tablecloths and serviettes, and a myriad of shiny silver cutlery, with a small flower and a tall candle in the middle.

They were led to a table in the centre, next to a window that looked out into the quaint little station, and the gentleman pulled out her chair for her before lighting the candle in the middle. Two other tables were occupied; one by an elderly couple, the other by a young couple who were looking at each other as starry eyed as Beth felt she kept staring at Caspian.

"We depart in fifteen minutes," he informed them. "And dinner will be served in half an hour. Can I get you a drink?"

Beth felt speechless, and glanced at the drinks menu to give herself time to collect her thoughts. It was so different from what she had been expecting - so wonderful - and although she was looking at the words in front of her, she found they weren't going in very successfully.

"Are you happy with wine?" Caspian asked, breaking the silence. "Or would you rather have something else?"

"Wine's good. White, please."

He ordered a bottle of white with a fancy sounding name that Beth didn't pay much attention to, as well as a jug of water, and once the waiter had slipped away to a different carriage, Beth met Caspian's eye across the table.

He was grinning broadly,a light in his eyes that was infectious.

"Wow," Beth said, grinning back. "An impressive second date, I'll say that."

"We've barely started," he said, looking younger somehow in his excitement.

"Where exactly are we going, then?"

"All around the area - ending up in Paignton, with a three-course dinner on the way, and I've been promised some amazing views."

Their wine arrived, and Beth took a sip, savouring how cold it was and the crisp taste, knowing she should take it slowly or she'd end up very quickly drunk. She felt tipsy already; intoxicated by her surroundings, by his thoughtfulness, by Caspian himself...

"Thank you, Caspian," she said, as they clinked glasses. "What an amazing idea."

Dinner was, of course, delicious, although Beth wasn't sure she would remember any of it afterwards. The views of Devon were breathtaking, bathed in the setting sun; glistening waters, waving palm trees (which she had not expected in this part of the world, and which Caspian later informed her were not actually palm trees, but very similar looking plants) and the sound of the steam engine as it chugged through the glorious surroundings. Wine flowed as easily as the conversation, and somehow they found themselves chugging through the English Riviera, sharing stories of their childhoods as if they had known one another for much longer than they had.

"My dad left when I was little," Beth admitted over the main course. "Ran off with his secretary, if you can believe the cliche. We've barely seen him since - to be honest, I don't even remember him that much. I think my sister does, a little more."

"So it was just you, your mum, and your sister?"

Beth nodded. "We're close, although like I said last time, mum can be hard work. She means well... But Lee, my sister, and I - we've always been close. Never argued too much. Although maybe if mum had someone else, she wouldn't feel the need to comment on every decision we make so heavily!"

Caspian smiled. "At least she cares."

"Oh, I know - I do try to remind myself of that regularly. Your mum sounds a little less forceful!"

"She has her moments, especially when grilling me about when I'm going to settle down and have a family."

"That one sounds familiar!"

"But it's just been the two of us for so long that we

haven't ever really fallen out."

Beth swirled the pasta on her fork, debating asking why there had only been the two of them; Cas carried on speaking without her needing to form the question that was hovering on her lips.

"Dad died when I was six," he said, a trace of emotion flickering through his eyes, although his voice remained steady. "Cancer. So then it was just me and mum."

"I'm sorry, Caspian," she said, reaching out without thinking and laying her hand across his.

"Like you said, it's hard to remember from that long ago, isn't it? But he was the love of mum's life, and she's never moved on. Maybe that's why she's always grilling me about my romantic life!"

Beth smiled. "It's nice you're still so close; I'm not sure I could do Sunday lunch every week with my mum, I have to say!"

The sky was turning a shade of violet by the time they had finished their dessert, polished off a second bottle of wine and been serenaded by a man and a guitar who had appeared in their carriage. Stars were just visible between clouds which strayed across the moon, and as the train pulled into the station at Paignton, Beth felt as though the whole evening had been a dream.

Caspian took her hand as they stood up, and headed into the slightly cooler night air. The clock on the station told them it was just after nine; and as it was a Sunday evening the town around them was fairly quiet.

"That was amazing," Beth said, stood beneath the archway that led into the station, one hand joined to Caspian's. "The best date I've ever been on."

"I aim to please," he said, that grin back on his face, his black hair catching the moon's light.

"You've definitely succeeded," she said, standing on tiptoes to press a brief kiss to his lips, a kiss that promised so much more, a kiss that merely hinted to the passion she knew they shared. "How do we get home?" she whispered, millimetres away from his lips.

CHAPTER TWENTY

Caspian grinned. "I booked a taxi - didn't think you'd fancy running back to Dartmouth…"

Beth laughed and their hands swung gently between them, clasped, as they began to walk in the direction of a waiting taxi. "You thought right," Beth agreed. "Amazing date or not, expecting me to run home from it might have ruined the effect somewhat."

"Not even I would fancy running home tonight, I promise," he said, opening the back door of the navy taxi that was waiting for them, before joining her in the back. He greeted the taxi driver as if he knew him, but didn't say a destination; the driver began travelling down the dark roads that led back to Dartmouth without needing direction.

Caspian glanced at his watch. "See," he said, turning to face Beth. "I told you I'd have you home for a respectable time. You can be in bed by ten at this rate."

Beth blushed a little, although he gave no hint whether he meant his words to have the suggestive tone that she was reading into them.

"You do stick to your word," she said, moistening her

lips a little and feeling his eyes on her in the dark rear of the car.

"Always."

They were silent for a few moments, just the quiet noise from the radio breaking the crackle of tension that seemed to build between them whenever they were close to one another.

"Where are you jetting off to this week, then?" Beth finally asked, as they started down the hill that led into Dartmouth.

"London, for most of the week," he said, "I have to leave first thing in the morning. Sometimes I go Sunday night…"

Beth smiled into the darkness. "Thanks for staying."

"It really is my pleasure."

"So you need an early night yourself, then?" she asked, feeling like it had been far too long since she had felt his lips on hers, felt the fireworks course through her veins.

"I can survive on very little sleep," he said.

"That's good to know. Can I see where you live?" She didn't know if it was the darkness, the desire, or the wine that was making her bold, but she felt like with Caspian she could be straight; she was sure he could feel the energy between them as much as she could.

A brief word to the driver and they changed their destination to the neighbouring village of Strete. Beth gasped slightly as she felt Caspian's fingers trail lightly across her knee; even through the black denim, there was just something about his touch. Barely there, and yet so full of promise...

The journey to Caspian's felt like an eternity, despite the fact that it only took a few minutes. Strete was only small, and she knew they had to drive past the beach where they'd first met to get there, although the dark skies stopped her seeing much of the view.

It was a little white house that they pulled up outside, semi-detached with four very symmetrical looking windows. Caspian paid the driver as Beth got out, glancing down the street at the very neat, ordered little row of houses.

"Home sweet home," Caspian said, putting his key in the lock and opening the door to let Beth inside first. "Not quite as exciting as living above a chip shop, I'm afraid..."

He flicked the light on and she saw him smile; there was clearly no offence meant. "No, this is very you," she said, wandering through to the room on the right which looked to be a living room. There was a neat stack of magazines on the coffee table; a white sofa with a black throw folded across one arm; and a large bookshelf in the corner. Not a stray mug or glass to be seen!

"What does very 'me' mean?" he asked.

"Oh, you know," Beth said with a grin on her face. "Ordered. Organised. Set in its ways..."

"Think you've got me all figured out, do you?" he asked as he moved to the kitchen in the next room, getting out a bottle of red and two glasses. "Think I'm so predictable?"

"I think you're anything but predictable, Caspian," she said with a sultry smile, enjoying feel of the name on her tongue. "And you are still quite an enigma." She took a glass of wine from him without a word and sipped it before finishing her thought. "But I do think that you like things to be organised, planned..."

Caspian smiled, a slight redness to his lips from where the wine had touched them, and gave a half nod. "I suppose you're right, although where you and I fit into that normally rigid pattern, I don't know - Elizabeth." It seemed he enjoyed using her given name as much as she did his.

Beth couldn't resist. She leaned in and kissed that wine from his lips - only a brief kiss at first, a brushing of her lips to his, the touch of her tongue against the fruitiness of the red wine - and then it wasn't so brief. Wine glasses somehow made it to the counter top without toppling all over the floor, and hands were in hair, lips were pressed together, bodies that been thrumming with energy throughout the evening finally touching.

"I like the spontaneity," Beth said, breathless, when for a moment their lips pulled apart.

"Me too," Caspian said, his chest rising and falling as rapidly as hers. And then his lips were against her neck, and everything seemed to become a haze of clothes, limbs and those delicious fireworks...

The alarm went off at an ungodly hour, and when Beth

opened her eyes from what felt like a night of no sleep - something which wasn't too far from the truth, in fact - she could see through the un-closed curtains that it wasn't even properly light yet. She glanced over at Caspian's dark-haired form sprawled on the pillow next to her, his eyes still closed, for a few seconds - when she realised the sound was coming from her own phone, and not Caspian's alarm clock. (Who even had an actual alarm clock these days? She was sure she hadn't seen one since she was a kid.) Beth leant over the side of the bed and rooted around in the clothes on the floor to find her bag, where her phone languished on 6% battery. It was far too early for her alarm - and far too early for the call that she realised was creating the noise to be good news.

Lee's name flashed up on the screen and Beth felt a lump in her throat.

"Hello? Lee?" she said, regardless of the sleeping body next to her.

"Beth-" came Lee's frantic voice through the speaker. "Beth, we're on our way to the hospital." Beth could hear the panic bubbling through her sister's normally calm and measured voice. "Holly's hit her head, there's a massive lump - they're worried about concussion. Oh god, Beth, I only turned my back for a second-"

"It's not your fault. It's going to be okay." Beth could hear James' voice in the background, sounding calmer than she suspected he was.

"I'll meet you there," Beth said, getting out of bed and throwing her clothes on as best as she could with one hand, not even noticing Caspian watching her. "I'll be as quick as I can."

"You don't have to Beth, I don't even know why I called you, I just-" Beth could hear tears cutting off her sister's words.

"Lee. I'm coming. It'll be okay, I'm sure. Kids are tough. Look, my phone's going to die - let me ring work and I'll be straight down there. I love you."

"Love you Beth." The line was disconnected, and Beth looked in dismay at the screen - 2%. That wasn't going to get her very far. Never mind the fact that she didn't have a car there, and she had a headache from the wine and the lack of sleep, and that she needed to get hold of work...

"Is everything okay?" Caspian asked, cutting through her panicked brain rambling.

"No, that was my sister - my niece has had an accident, they're having to go to the hospital, I need to meet her there - but I need to call work, and get home, and-"

Caspian began to pull on his own clothes. "Why don't I take you to the hospital? It'll be quicker, and you can get home with your sister, right?"

Beth nodded. "But you've got to dash off..."

"I can juggle things, don't worry. Besides - this is earlier than even my alarm goes off." He reached across the bed and took her hand, giving a half smile. "It'll be okay. They're always overly cautious with kids, but like you said, they're tough. Let's get you there so you can help your sister, and I'm sure by this afternoon you'll all be home and catching up on sleep."

"I hope so," Beth said. "Thanks, Cas, I really appreciate it. You don't have to..." She suddenly felt like things were a little formal - the news was so far out of their little bubble of fireworks, dates and great spontaneous sex that she didn't really know how to act. There was a moment's silence, then he reached out his hand.

"Let me charge your phone. I just need to throw a few things in a bag for work - use mine to call your work, then we can get going."

"Mr. Practical," she said with a small smile, and then did as she was told.

"I feel bad just dashing off," Caspian said as they pulled up outside the hospital, the sky finally light, filled with a cheery sunshine that didn't feel like it fitted in.

"Cas, you didn't even need to drive me here - honestly, I completely understand you need to get to London."

"Will you let me know how she is?"

Beth was touched that he cared. "Of course. Now you go - I'll be in touch."

"Me too . Beth, as much as I love the spontaneity, I also really need to know I'm going to see you again."

His eyes met hers and there was a rawness there she hadn't seen before; like he was admitting something he found very difficult to voice. For a second she pressed her lips to his, and then pulled away. "You will. I promise. Have a good trip - don't forget about me while you're gone."

"Not possible," he said, and then she was gone, disappearing through the hospital doors, and he was on the road once more.

It didn't take Beth long to find them; the A&E department was small and thankfully not too busy. Lee was sat on the bed, Holly sat in her crossed legs, a sizeable bump on her head and looking a little sorry for herself. James paced the small curtained area, but found a smile for Beth as he saw her approaching.

"Beth, you didn't have to come," he said, giving his sister—in-law to-be a brief hug.

"Benefits of living so close," she said, reaching Lee for a hug. "I can come and support you if you need it. What happened? What are they saying?"

"They want to monitor her for a while - they called us in because she was throwing up," James answered. "But that seems to have stopped now. They don't seem overly panicked, but with her being so young, and the size of the bump..."

"We were in kitchen," Lee cut over her husband. "She was crawling on the floor, I turned round to grab a glass of water and the next thing I knew she was screaming. Somehow she'd rolled over while crawling and hit her head on corner of the kitchen island." Tears began rolling down her cheeks. "And then she was sick, and I called 111 and they wanted us to get straight down here. I'm sorry,

Beth, I shouldn't have rung, I just panicked, and you're missing work and-"

"Shirley Davis," Beth said, knowing her use of her full name would at least get her sister's attention. "It's fine. I'm here, and if it's absolutely nothing and little Holly is just a bit grumpy for a few days - which I'm sure is all it will be — then all the better. You never need to feel bad about ringing me."

Lee gently stroked her daughter's hair, avoiding the bump. "When did you get to be so wise and commanding?" she asked.

"Always have been, sis - you were just too busy being the responsible one to notice!"

She's being monitored at home but seems like she's fine :) x Beth text Caspian once she was at home and had been able to charge her phone to a decent percentage. There was a message from work telling her not to worry and just to let them know about the next day, and one from Caspian, checking in that everything was all right.

It was dinner time when Beth eventually got back to her little flat, dropped off by her sister and almost-brother-in-law (who were thankfully, and understandably, too preoccupied with their daughter's wellbeing to ask how she had got to the hospital without her car). Still in her clothes from their date the night before, and suffering from a serious lack of sleep, she grabbed fish and chips from the shop - ignoring Sam's jibes about her being out all night - and took them to bed to eat. With a quick message to Lee, telling her to let her know if anything changed, and one to work to say she would be in tomorrow, she got into her comfiest pyjamas and, not caring how early it was, sunk into her bed for some much-need beauty sleep.

CHAPTER TWENTY-ONE

Can you be spontaneous this weekend? I'll have you back in time for Sunday lunch with your mum - promise. Beth x

She bit her lip as she pressed send. In the two weeks since Holly's thankfully long-forgotten trip to the hospital, she and Caspian had exchanged texts but had not seen each other. He'd not made it back from London the previous weekend, and so they had a vague plan to go on a date this weekend - although after the romantic steam train ride, Beth had decided she ought to make a plan. And that she was going to go all out...

You know me, Mr Spontaneous. Does this mean I need to pack my pyjamas? X

She grinned at the quick response, and couldn't resist a cheeky one in return.

Not sure you'll need them... but yes, overnight stay. I'll pick you up Saturday morning, 9ish? X

You've got me very intrigued...

Beth laughed, and checked her watch - nearly the end of her lunch break, and she needed to make sure everything was organised for the weekend as soon as possible. With the yearly Dartmouth Regatta in full swing, the whole area was teeming with even more holiday-makes than normal, and she knew she had a packed afternoon of tours around the house and the gardens.

Good :)

❖ ❖ ❖

She saw him looking out of the window as she pulled up outside his perfectly ordered house. She smiled and lifted a hand to wave as she turned the engine off and pushed her sunglasses to sit on top of her head. The September sunshine streamed through the windows and she was ecstatic that the weather had lasted past the August bank holiday weekend. It would have been too expensive and too busy to follow her plans that weekend and so she had hoped that once the kids were back in school, and the holidaymakers had gone home, that the weather would still be nice enough for the weekend trip. She was not disappointed.

She got out of the car but it wasn't really necessary; he was ready and exiting the door before she even reached it. With a small blue holdall in one hand and his own sunglasses in another, he lent over to give her a brief kiss that, as usual, left her wanting more.

"Morning," he said and she smiled.

"Good morning. Ready for an adventure?"

"I'm slightly nervous, if truth be told," he said, although the sparkle in his eyes suggested his words were a lie.

"It's my turn to be mysterious," Beth said with a laugh, "and your turn to wonder. Come on, we've got a bit of a drive." She watched as he bent his tall frame into her small car and then jumped in the driver's seat herself.

"Coffee?" she asked, gesturing to two takeaway cups in the cup holders at the front of the car.

"Very organised - thank you." He took a sip.

"No need to sound so surprised - just because I'm spontaneous doesn't mean I can't be organised."

"I never said that! Those words are all yours." In truth, it had been a rather last-minute decision; as she left through the fish and chip shop, she'd noticed the takeaway cups on the side and grabbed a couple before running back upstairs to make herself a cup of tea and Cas a coffee for the journey. It was a two-hour drive and she didn't want to stop - that would only take away from the time they would have on their little trip.

"So, any hints about where we're going?" he asked, one hand on the handle above the door. Beth smiled slightly; she might have guessed he would be a nervous passenger.

"No hints," she said, "Other than the one I sent last night."

"Ah, yes." Caspian grinned! I've got my swimming trunks as instructed - but the real question is, have you got your bikini? I seem to remember you not needing one..."

Beth tapped Caspian lightly on the knee and laughed. "No more information. You'll just have to wait and see -

and try to relax, will you, my driving is not that bad - I promise!"

Caspian looked a little sheepish and let go of the handle. "I like being in control," he admitted with a shrug.

"I know that - but it's good to let go sometimes. Trust me!"

"I do," he said, and his words were laced with sincerity. He tried to relax as they set off down the A38. "Well, there's not much this way other than Cornwall - so is that a good guess?"

Beth nodded. "Well I can't deny geography gives something away - yes, Cornwall is our destination, but it's a pretty big county and that's the last information I'm giving!"

Caspian laughed, a light-hearted sound that made Beth's lips turn to an even wider smile. It had been a while since she had seen the grumpy, aloof Caspian she had met on the beach. He seemed to be enjoying himself every time they met - and she felt exactly the same way.

"Your mum didn't mind me whisking away for the weekend, then?" she asked.

"You make me sound like a teenager who has to get permission!"

"You know what I mean," she said.

"No she didn't - I did promise that you'd have me back for lunch on Sunday though, like you said!" He paused. "She was a bit surprised though, I think."

"Surprised that you're going away for the weekend

with someone you've only known a few weeks? Maybe she thinks I'm going to kidnap you."

He laughed once more. "I don't think it's kidnap she's worried about - although she's very intrigued about who you are." Beth blushed, secretly pleased he'd been talking about her to his mum. "No, just surprised because it is rather out of character for me - as I'm sure you have guessed."

"My mum on the other hand wouldn't be at all surprised if I told her about our plans," Beth said with a sigh. "I'm not sure she'd think it was responsible, but she wouldn't be surprised!"

"Mothers love me," he said, with an air of arrogance that made Beth giggle.

"I bet they do."

"Seriously - ten minutes with me and I bet she'd think you whisking me off to god-knows-where is a fantastic idea!"

"Oh you certainly think a lot of yourself, don't you! Within ten minutes of meeting my sister's fiancé for the first time, I think she'd learnt that Lee was expecting - so I think you'd be winning for first impressions." She indicated at the roundabout, then realised how her words might have sounded and tried hard to take them back. "Not that I'm suggesting, or saying-"

"Relax, Beth," Caspian said in his chocolaty deep voice. "I'm not taking it as a proposal."

Beth laughed to cover her embarrassment. Here was a guy she'd been on a few dates with - and yes, thought about a lot, and yes, slept with on a couple of occasions - and she was letting her mouth ramble on without any sort of screening process.

And she couldn't even blame it on alcohol.

It was just gone eleven when they pulled up outside the little cottage overlooking Fistral beach in Newquay. The view took Beth's breath away, which she was extremely pleased about - it had taken a decent chunk of her limited finances to pay for a night here, even out of the season. She was glad to see it looked worth every penny.

"Newquay," Caspian said with a smile. "I haven't been here since I was a little boy."

Beth grinned. "Good surprise?"

"Great surprise."

Caspian grabbed both their bags while Beth went to find the key safe she had been told would be by the side of the house. Sure enough, there it was, partially obscured by ivy, and she let them into the cute little one-bedroom.

It was simply decorated with a nautical theme clearly in mind; a blue sofa and a television were in the living room, with white walls dotted with seascapes. An open plan kitchen was off to one side, with a breakfast bar and two stools. Beth ran her fingers across the cool marble of the counter top where a welcome note and a cake had been left.

It was the garden, though, that had really made her decide to part with her hard-earned money for their night away. It was only small, with a neatly manicured lawn and a sprawling rose bush, but its views over the beach and sparkling ocean were breathtaking - and to top it all off, there was a hot tub situated in the perfect spot to enjoy those views.

"Wow," Caspian said, wrapping his arms around her waist from behind. "A pretty incredible - what is it, third date?"

She laughed. Somehow it was *only* their third date. "Well, I do like to win."

"I thought you liked our train ride?" Caspian said.

Beth turned around in the circle of his arms to face him. "It was perfect," she said. "Which is why I wanted to plan something incredible, too." She bit her lip, suddenly feeling a little unsure.

"Is it too much?" she asked. "Going to scare you away?" She was only half joking, although she tried to sound flippant.

Caspian lifted one hand from her waist and placed it on the side of her head, fixing her with a piercing stare that sent her heart fluttering and her skin tingling.

"Definitely not scaring me away," he said, with an intensity that made her shiver. He leant down until his lips brushed hers, holding them there for a fraction of a second as she pressed her body against his.

"If we start kissing, I can't promise we'll make it out of the house," he murmured. "And as you've driven us all the way down here…"

Beth sighed, and then placed a hand on his chest, lightly pushing him away.

"You're right - as usual," she said.

"You know me so well already," he said with a slight smirk.

In her head, Beth disagreed - he still seemed such a mystery to her in so many ways. But she said nothing, and instead looked at her watch; "Grab your trunks - we've got somewhere to be in less than twenty minutes."

"I am exhausted," said Beth, lying on the beach in her black bikini, wringing water out of her hair. Caspian lay next to her, his body flecked with droplets of water, his tanned skin seeming to glow in the bright sunlight.

"Me too," he said with a grin, but Beth certainly felt that he didn't look quite as worn out as she did.

"If I'd known you were going to be so much better at surfing than me, I'm not sure I would have booked the lesson!" She laughed; "You've really never done it before?"

He shook his head, sending a few errant droplets flying in Beth's direction. "No, but I loved it. What a thrill! Amazing plan, Elizabeth."

Beth didn't even pause to cringe at the name. "Maybe for those of us who didn't spend most of the time under the water..."

Caspian ran a hand along her thigh, causing the flesh

to prickle, despite Beth being anything but cold. "You stayed up at the end!"

"For about a minute," Beth said, but her eyes were bright and sparkling, and she felt exhilarated.

Caspian rolled over onto his front and threw an arm across her waist. "Thanks, Beth - I've had an amazing morning."

She grinned broadly, trailing her fingers across his arm. It was so new to be able to touch him whenever she wanted, to feel the electricity when her skin brushed against his... "Well, for a man who is named for a sea and swims in the sea every night, I figured it was a pretty safe bet. And our weekend's only just beginning..."

He kissed her lazily, feeling more calm and free than he had felt in years.

Beth felt like she could stay there forever, the warm sand sticking to her back, her salty skin pressed so deliciously against his...

If she weren't so hungry,

"Lunch?" Caspian asked, and she had a sneaking suspicion that he had heard her stomach rumble.

"An excellent plan!"

After fresh crab sandwiches, which they ate sat outside the little café overlooking the water, Beth dragged Caspian to an ice cream van.

"Come on, you're on holiday. You can have ice cream with me, Mr Healthy!"

"Hmmm," he said, pretending to deliberate. "I guess the surfing was exercise..."

"Most definitely. And you can exercise more later..."

Caspian raised his eyebrows with a cheeky grin. Beth laughed so loudly the children in front turned to look at her, and she shoved Caspian out of the line. "I meant a night time swim, if you want to!"

"Sure you did."

"You've got a filthy mind," she said quietly, to avoid the censure of the parents in front. Caspian was saved from responding by the man in the truck asking for their order.

They wandered across the sand with an ice cream each, weaving in and out of the various groups sat on towels, rugs and folding chairs on the busy beach. When Cas took his free hand and entwined his fingers with hers, Beth smiled and lost track of what they had been saying.

They walked like that for a while, enjoying their ice creams, the sound of the waves and the feel of their hands wrapped together. Beth had kept the wet bikini on under her dress, but the sunshine had quickly dried it out and she felt comfortable in the late summer heat.

"So," Caspian said, as they reached a wall and decided to lean against it. "Is this a standard Beth Davis move then? Third date and a trip away?"

"What's that supposed to mean?" Beth glanced at him, struggling a little to read his tone.

He threw the end of his cornet down the beach, where seagulls hungrily jumped on it, and used his now free hand to tuck a strand of hair behind her ear. "I mean... is this something that you would normally do? Or is it... different?" He couldn't seem to get out what he was trying to say. Every word sounded a little like an insult. "Oh, this really isn't coming out right..."

Beth hesitated, before posing her own question in return. "Do you plan romantic steam train rides for all the women you take on second dates?"

Caspian's smile suddenly seemed shy; she felt like there was a flash of what he might have looked like younger, without the air of mystery that she sensed around him. "I rarely take a woman on a second date," he admitted. "And when I do, it's usually a meal at a local restaurant."

"Well, I don't make a habit of going away with men on a third date, no. Is that a problem?"

Caspian shook his head emphatically. "What I mean is... this feels different, right? For both of us?"

Beth felt the slightly prickly exterior that she had erected at his questions softening. "I told you that night in the pub," she said softly. "Fireworks, baby."

She felt something buzzing between them as their eyes locked, felt like the beach could have emptied around them and she wouldn't have noticed. This was certainly different than anything she'd embarked on in a long time - probably ever. She'd never been so excited before to plan a weekend away; never thought so much about what would suit the other person, what would make him smile. It had been a long time since her thoughts had wandered so frequently to a man, and she definitely didn't feel like this was only a third date.

"IS there a plan for the rest of the afternoon?" he asked, not taking his eyes off hers.

"Not until this evening."

"I've got an idea." He took her hand and Beth felt in that moment that she was very much in danger of losing her heart to this handsome man.

She smiled to herself; maybe it was about time she lost her heart. As long as she had his in return.

CHAPTER TWENTY-TWO

They found themselves in the centre of town, weaving through groups of people, hand-in-hand. The September sunshine still felt warm as the afternoon carried on, and they window-shopped as they chatted. Caspian pulled her down a side street and placed a kiss on the side of her head, then stopped outside a pink and black building.

"Aha," he said. "I thought it was here!"

Beth looked up at the sign above it: *Aurora Books.*

"I remember reading about a little bookshop in New-quay that had been here for years and stocked all sorts of old and rare books," he said, answering her questioning look. "And here it is!"

"You just happened to read about a bookshop in New-quay?"

"I work with a lot of people in publishing, remember - there's a lot of magazines lying around in offices that talk about this sort of thing! Anyway, I thought you'd like it."

She grinned; it was a great idea. As they entered a bell rang and she breathed in the slightly musty smell of old books. The shop was quite dark, with rows and rows of bookshelves and several customers perusing old-looking volumes. A middle-aged woman sat behind the counter, reading a book herself, only seeming to stop if she absolutely had to serve somebody.

Beth loved it.

They wandered down a row of shelves, trying to figure out how the books were organised (Beth wasn't sure they were at all), and pulling out interesting looking tomes. When they spoke it was in hushed voices; the bookshop certainly had the feel of a library.

"How's your writing going?" Caspian asked, and Beth was touched he remembered.

"To be honest," she said, feeling a little guilty, "I've been a bit distracted."

"By what?" he asked, although she was fairly sure he knew.

"Oh, I don't know," she said, stroking her fingers down the faded spine of a copy of *Peter Pan.* "There's this handsome man I met swimming in the sea, who takes me on steam train rides and kisses me in empty shop doorways..."

Caspian laughed, and earned himself a sharp look from the proprietor. Definitely a library atmosphere. "Sounds terrible."

"Oh, it is," Beth said with a grin.

"Seriously, though, I wouldn't want to distract you from your writing. Handsome or not..." He paused. "You seemed so excited about it."

"I am," she said, moving over to the next row of books. "And I am still writing a bit. But you're right - less time spent in your bed, more time writing."

"Well, I didn't quite say that..." He pulled out an old-looking copy of an Agatha Christie book and passed it to Beth, sure she'd be interested. "But I'd love to read it, once you're done."

Beth smiled, both at the book and his comment, and didn't answer. She wasn't quite sure how she felt about anyone reading her scribblings...

Two hours passed by quite happily, and before they knew it the shop was closing and they had five books between them to purchase. Had she not known how low her bank balance was in danger of running, Beth would have bought more, but she was happy with the two Agatha Christie novels she'd ended up with as they strolled out of the shop. The shops were emptying as they wandered back towards the cottage they were staying in, but the pubs were filling up, and they passed cheerful looking beer gardens filled with people enjoying a pint and the September sunshine.

"Do you enjoy working at Greenway, then?" he asked as they meandered up the hill.

"I do," Beth said, giving the question a little thought before answering further. "And I know it's no great career, and that I'm barely earning above minimum wage, but the place is gorgeous, the history is fascinating and it inspires me to write. I feel so much more excited to get up every day and go to work than I've felt in any other job I've been in. " She blushed. "Sorry, you probably didn't need that much information in answer to a simple question!"

When Caspian smiled, she noticed a slight dimple around his lips, and she marvelled at how young and carefree he could look in one moment, and so brooding and concerned the next. "As long as you're happy in a job, I don't think it matters what it is - and like you said, it gives you the chance to be creative, too."

"And what about your job?" she asked. "It sounds very important and stressful - do you enjoy it?"

He too seemed to consider his answer before giving it; she wondered if anyone had ever asked it. "Yes," he said. "I think I do. I'm good at it - if that doesn't sound too arrogant - and I know what I'm doing. I don't find it too stressful, although the travelling backwards and forwards can be a bit exhausting. But sometimes I get the train, which is nicer, and the sea views when you go through Dawlish always make me feel like the journey is worth it." They reached the top of the hill and both glanced back to look at the setting sun sparkling on the ocean. "Sorry, I'm rambling."

"I like to hear you talk," she said with a soft smile. "Do you ever consider just living in London or wherever permanently? Just coming to Devon on holidays?"

"Do you think I should?"

Beth shook her head, afraid to admit on a third date - although a rather unconventional one - that she really would not want him to move away. "No, but I'm guessing you've considered it?"

"I have," he said, as they continued round the corner to the cottage. "And my mum insists I don't need to live down here for her. To be honest, I'm not just in London - I travel around a fair bit to other cities, so even if I did live there, it's not like I would be able to stop travelling all together."

"But you'd be a hell of a lot more central there than living in Devon," she said, unsure why she was giving him reasons to move away.

"It definitely sounds like you're looking for reasons to get rid of me!"

She shook her head. "Just trying to understand..."

"I'm not sure I understand myself most of the time," Caspian admitted. "So I'm afraid I don't think you'll have much luck. But please, feel free to keep trying!"

"Oh, I plan to," she said with a grin. "Now, I think it's about time we tried out that hot tub..."

As Beth was still wearing her swimming costume under her dress, she skipped straight out into the secluded little garden and, waiting for Caspian to join her, peeled off the dress and let it drop to the floor.

"Are you trying to seduce me?" Caspian asked with a cheeky grin.

Beth shook her head. "Me? Never. I'm just getting into the hot tub to enjoy the sunset. Are you going to join me?"

He nodded. "Give me two minutes."

Beth slipped in to the hot bubbles alone, facing out so she could see the expanse of the ocean as the orange and red sunlight hit it on its way down. The day had been exhilarating so far, and she wasn't sure she could ever remember having so much fun with someone she was dating. Her muscles ached after the surfing, along with the walking they had done that day, and she enjoyed letting the warm water soothe them.

It didn't take long for Caspian to reappear. He had changed back into his trunks - an event Beth was sad she had missed - and was carrying two glasses of wine.

"Where did that appear from?" Beth asked, reaching out to take one as he climbed into the water beside her.

"Does it sound bad if I told you I brought it with me?"

Beth laughed. "Do you always bring wine away with you?"

He shook his head, looking a little bashful. "Honestly? I was a bit nervous about the weekend. And since every date we've been on has included wine..."

"You thought it would make things less awkward?"

He nodded.

"And is that why you've brought it out here?"

He shook his head. "I haven't felt awkward for a second. I'm just not really used to going away with anyone..."

She took a sip of the crisp white wine and let out a contented sigh. "So why did you bring the wine out now?"

He shrugged. "I just thought if I was going to enjoy a beautiful view, with a beautiful woman, it would be made even nicer with a cold glass of wine."

"Now I think you're trying to seduce me," Beth said.

"Always."

The view and the wine really were gorgeous, but they were quickly forgotten. Their wine glasses were placed on the side of the tub, barely touched, as they moved closer in the water. The teasing words, and a day of being physically so close to one another was clearly having an effect, and Beth felt as though sparks were jumping from her skin. She let Caspian take the lead as his fingers trailed down her bare arm, making her shiver in spite of the warm water surrounding her. They had not stopped talking all day, but now they fell silent, absorbing themselves in the feeling of the cool evening air on their skin, the warmth of the bubbles and the electricity from their touching bodies. Beth wasn't sure who moved first, but when their lips were almost connected, she felt his hand on her waist pulling her closer, before his lips pressed to hers and she felt her body melt into his. Her ams wrapped around his neck and her legs around his waist, closing the space between them as he ran his lips down the side of her neck.

"Beth," he murmured, and the sound of her name on his lips made her groan.

"Caspian," she whispered, pulling his lips back to hers for another kiss that felt like explosions were going off around her.

It was only when she pulled away to take a breath that she realised it wasn't just the kiss; there really were fireworks going off in the sky above her. Blue, green, red flashes, each reflected in the calm ocean below them, the moon and the dark sky the only indicator of the amount of time they had spent kissing in that hot tub.

"They're really there, right?" Caspian whispered into her ear. "Not a figment of my imagination brought on by your lips?"

Beth couldn't help but laugh. She turned herself to face them, not moving from his lap, and they watched together as the lights exploded in the sky and then fell dramatically to the ocean below. "No, I'm definitely seeing the fireworks too."

The bright lights and explosions, however, could not distract either of them from the proximity of their bodies, from the promise of what they had started.

"Have you got a towel?" Caspian asked, and Beth shook her head.

"You know me," she said. "Always spontaneous, never prepared."

"I feel like that pays off sometimes!" he said with a laugh. "I think we're going to have to make a run for the bedroom then, stop us freezing once we hit that night air..."

"Think we can make it to the bedroom?" Beth asked, a sparkle in her eye as the last firework fizzled out in the air.

Caspian took her hand and pulled her up, and they

tried not to knock over the wine glasses as they dashed into through the double doors, the cold air making their previously warm skin prickle. Beth was shrieking by the time they'd made it into the bedroom, a room she hadn't seen when they arrived. It was simple again, with a blue and white checked duvet on a double bed, and two matching nightstands, with a large clock above the door.

"We're booked in for dinner in half an hour," she said, a little breathless.

Caspian reached round to click the clasp of her bikini, letting it fall to floor. "I think we're going to be a little late..."

◆ ◆ ◆

Beth stretched out her arms on the white pillows and smiled at Caspian lying next to her.

"Worth being late for dinner for?" he asked, propping his head up on his arm.

"Oh, I think so... but we really should ring them if we want a table still!"

"I need a shower first," Caspian said, with a stretch of his tanned arms.

"Me too," said Beth, watching as he got out of bed without a stitch on. She was a little more shy and kept the blue checked duvet cover over her body as she sat up.

"Want to join me?" Caspian asked with a cheeky grin.

Beth laughed; "I'm not sure that's the quickest option... but who am I to argue! Let me just ring the restaurant."

A quick phone call and a not so quick shower later, and they were both dressed and ready to head out. Caspian wore his black jeans with a crisp white shirt that he left open at the collar and Beth found her eye drawn to the patch where his tanned skin contrasted so deliciously with the shirt. She wore a summery blue dress covered in butterflies with a pair of flat shoes; after all the walking they'd done today, not to mention their surfing and *other* activities, there was no way she fancied wearing a pair of heels. Besides, they would be walking to and from the restaurant since it was not that far - and the views were spectacular, and the weather so pleasant.

As soon as they left the cottage, Caspian took hold of her hand, and she smiled at how quickly the gesture felt natural.

"What a perfect day," she said as they strolled down the hill back towards the beach. "I mean, I don't like brag about my date-planning-"

Caspian interrupted her "No, you should do- it has been an amazing day. An amazing date!" He paused to kiss her and she marveled at how spectacular things really were turning out. Who could have known, two short months ago when she complained in a nightclub that she couldn't find the fireworks, that her life could change so drastically.

CHAPTER TWENTY-THREE

Beth had spent a while on her lunch breaks at work researching different restaurants in the area. This one had great reviews and great views, and so it had seemed like the obvious choice. Floor to ceiling windows looked out over the ocean, which was only just still visible. Although they were late, they were seated quickly and were soon enjoying cocktails as they looked out over the bay. Beth smiled at the sight of Caspian drinking the pink and orange creation with an umbrella; it seemed so at odds with his stern exterior.

"How's your niece?" he asked.

"Fine, thanks, or so my sister tells me when we talk - running her ragged apparently, so she's clearly recovered from her trip to A&E!"

"Did you say she'd moved to the area fairly recently?"

"Last Christmas. It was all rather sudden and out of character!" Beth sipped her drink, mindful that having already had wine and not much to eat, it was liable to go straight to her head.

"Now I am intrigued!"

"She was a lawyer in Bristol," Beth said, taking another sip of her cocktail, which tasted dangerously non-alcoholic since she'd seen the amount of alcohol that had gone into it. "Married to a doctor. Then she walked in one day to find him sleeping with some blonde from work. In their bed."

"Scumbag," Caspian said - a response Beth heartily approved of.

"Indeed. So she came to Totnes, to get her head together, then ended up buying a café..."

"She bought a café?" Caspian looked a little incredulous.

"Yep. Found a flat share, planned to go back to Bristol once she'd got herself together. Then she met a handsome police officer..." Beth grinned. "Fell in love, fell pregnant and they're getting married this Christmas!"

"Wow," Caspian said. "Talk about spontaneous..."

Beth laughed. "The funny thing is, before that she was so predictable. Everything organised, five-year plan, hell, probably a ten-year plan!" She paused; "A bit like you, really."

"I'm not sure I have things as planned out as you imagine..."

"You are a bit of an enigma," she said, tucking into her meal that she had barely noticed arriving.

"Does she still practise law?" Caspian asked between

mouthfuls.

"She's started again on the side - although how she has time with a ten-month-old and a café, I don't know."

"Can I meet her?"

The question surprised Beth. When had she last introduced a guy to her family? It was certainly a rare occurrence. And this was only a third date.

But...

"Do you want to?"

"Yeah. If you'd be happy for me to."

"Okay. We can go for coffee sometime."

Caspian smiled.

"Can I meet your mum?" Beth asked, feeling like that was a further leap forward - but that if she didn't ask now, it might be a very long time before she felt she could. And she was very intrigued to meet his mother, the woman who kept him anchored in this small town.

"You've already met my mum," Caspian said, and Beth felt he was stalling for time.

"As a tour guide. Not as." She reached around for the word that described this deliciously intense *thing* between them. "Not as someone you're dating."

"My mum's not met anyone I've dated since I was sixteen."

"How old are you now?"

"Thirty-one," he answered.

"Surely she's had enough time to get over the last one then?"

He gave a short, sharp laugh. "She was a goth with a pierced lip and black lipstick," Caspian said. "I'm not sure she'd ever say she was over it!"

"Teenage rebellious phase?"

Something like that," he said, emptying the rest of his glass. "But yes, if you want to, you can meet my mum."

Beth grinned. "Good."

When the bill was brought to the table, the waitress automatically placed it in front of Cas, which irritated Beth. She reached across to grab it, but before she could, he placed his hand over hers.

"Let me get this."

"I invited you in the date, I pay. That's the way it works," Beth insisted.

"But when dates are as epic as this," he said, reaching into his pocket for his wallet with his other hand, "It's only fair we split some of the cost. Please?"

She didn't know whether it was his plea, his compliment or the look in his eyes as they met hers, but her ire cooled and she withdrew her hand.

"Okay. If you insist." If truth be told, the whole weekend had been rather expensive, and a little help wouldn't go amiss.

Hand-in-hand they strolled across the beach, which was now bathed in the inky light of the night sky, reflections of the moon bouncing off the water and making it glint and shimmer before them. The sand was cooler now, and Beth took off her shoes to feel it between her toes, despite Caspian laughing at her.

"When you don't grow up by the sea, you appreciate these things more!" she insisted. "I feel like I'm in a movie."

The alcohol and the perfection of the day had left her feeling a little giddy, and she added occasional skips to her step as they traversed the almost deserted beach. It looked completely different than it had earlier in the day, but Beth thought it was possibly even more beautiful.

"Tell me something," Caspian said, watching her intently.

"Tell you what?"

"Something about you. Something other people don't know."

Beth thought for a moment, finding it a little harder to put her thoughts into words than she had done before the alcohol. "Okay," she said. "But you've got to promise not to judge me."

"Now I am intrigued..."

Beth paused and glanced at him. "I've never voted."

"What? How is that possible?"

She put her head in her free hand and groaned. "I

know, I know, it's awful! I'm really ashamed of it, which is why no-one else knows." Why she had decided to tell Caspian that little fact was beyond her, but there it was, out in the open. "My sister would kill me if she knew!"

"Well, at least you feel bad about it," Caspian said with a grin.

"It started off with not caring, when I was younger. Then I just didn't know who to vote for, and didn't want to fall into the trap of just voting the way my mum does, and now here I am, twenty-eight and never voted."

Caspian shook his head. "It's important to vote, make your voice heard."

"I know, I know, I do feel bad about it! Look, I promise next time there's an election, I'll do my research and vote, okay?"

"Good."

"Your turn," Beth said; "Tell me something nobody else knows."

He paused, clearly thinking through his answer, and Beth watched the reflection of the moonlight shimmer on the black ocean as they walked in a pleasant silence. The air had cooled off a little although it was not unpleasant; without discussing it they turned and started to walk back in the direction of the cottage.

"I'm scared of ending up like my mum," he finally said, and the words seemed to have so much gravity that Beth stopped in her tracks and lifted her chin so she could look up into his dark eyes.

"What does that mean?" she asked, letting her fingers gently graze the stubble on his chin. "Old? On your own?"

"Heartbroken," he admitted, bravely maintaining their eye contact even though Beth could feel he wanted to look away.

"She lost the love of her life," Beth said, repeating words he'd said to her on that last date.

He nodded. "And she's never been the same since."

"Do you think, though, if you asked her, she'd rather have never loved him at all, to avoid the pain?"

He shook his head, with a sad smile on his lips. "No, I don't think so."

"'Tis better to have loved and lost than never to have loved at all," Beth said, pressing her lips to his for a moment, offering some sort of comfort she hoped to the pain he seemed to be feeling.

"Tennyson?" Caspian asked, and Beth nodded.

"I think - and this may be the cocktails talking," she said, trying to lighten the mood just a little, "But I think that's the price you have to be willing to pay for true love. I see my sister, and what she had with her first husband - that was never true love. What she's got now, I think that's the real deal - and she'd be devastated if she lost him. But I don't think you can think like that. Otherwise how would anyone ever fall in love? Have children? Be happy?"

"I think," Caspian said, "And this may be the cocktails

talking..."

Beth laughed.

"I think you're very wise. And in this moonlight, in the glow of this amazing day, you make my fears seem a little less scary."

She kissed him then - what else could she do with the heady mix of alcohol, soul-baring and chemistry that they were soaking in? She let her fingers glide to his hair, holding onto it tightly as their tongues met and reason was abandoned. His hand was on her back, pressing her closer, wiping away all thoughts and just leaving a burning trail of passion, and emotion, and desire.

It was very late that night when Beth lay wide awake in Caspian's arms as he softly snored. She had watched him sleeping for a while, presuming sleep would wash over her after how busy they had been that day, but it evaded her into the small hours. His confession was on her mind, and she realised that she tried to live her life without any fear, even if that wasn't always possible. It seemed he had lived his in fear for a long time, and that explained some of the mystery she felt surrounded him. She tried not to read into the fact that he was talking about love and heartbreak with her. It was all too soon; she couldn't be falling for this man so quickly, else she worried she might end up with the broken heart. It wasn't always possible to push the fear away...

Easing herself from his arms without waking him, she reached for her notebook which was buried at the bottom of her holdall. She had taken to having it on her at all times, in case inspiration struck, and she was pleased she had done so. She held her breath as she flicked on the side light, hoping it wouldn't wake Cas, and watched him for another moment or two as he steadily breathed in and out, his pattern unchanged by the intruding light.

She put pen to paper and let the words flow out, feeling Adrienne's longing and heartbreak keenly as she let inspiration take over and the rest of the story take shape.

CHAPTER TWENTY-FOUR

Beth awoke the next morning to the smell of bacon coming from the adjoining room. It took her a moment or two to figure out where she was, as the sunlight streamed in the large window and the sound of seagulls floated in. She grinned as it all came flooding back to her, and as she stretched in the empty bed she glanced up at the clock. It was gone eleven, which would have shocked her had she not been up until nearly five writing several chapters of her novel. She felt she was coming close to the end, and was excited about the prospect - although exhaustion had eventually got the better of her.

"Good morning, sleeping beauty." Caspian's cheerful voice greeted her as she padded into the kitchen, wearing his shirt over her underwear. He grinned at the sight, but didn't comment.

"Where did all this come from?" she asked, as he loaded up plates with bacon, eggs, toast and sausages.

"Well, I went for a run this morning-"

"You did what?" Beth laughed and took a seat. "Do you never stop?"

"You looked like you needed more sleep! Anyway, I went for a run and stopped to get some supplies on my way back. I hope I'm not ruining any date plans?"

Beth shook her head. "Nope - just one more place for us to go before we drive back, but there's no rush - shit, except your lunch with your mum!" In her exhaustion, she had forgotten all about her promise.

"Relax," he said, putting a plate in front of her and gently pushing her shoulder so she sat back down. "I rang my mum. Told her what a wonderful time I was having and promised to cook her a roast for dinner. So as long as I'm home by six, she won't hate you."

"I didn't plan to sleep in so late," Beth said, realising how famished she was and spreading liberal amounts of butter on her toast. "You could have woken me! I'm really sorry."

"It's okay, honest," Caspian said, bringing over a mug of tea for her and sitting to tuck in himself. "Didn't realise I'd exhausted you so much…"

She batted him lightly on the forearm and laughed. "Not to ruin your mood, but I actually stayed up ridiculously late writing. Inspiration struck…"

Caspian grinned. "That's great! Can I read it?"

"When it's done," Beth promised. "You can be the first, I promise."

"I'll hold you to that."

The last stop on their little tour was an art gallery overlooking the ocean that Beth had read about when researching the area. Like so many places around, the exterior was made largely of glass, to make the most of the beautiful vistas in the area.

They wandered quietly, and Beth wondered if he was feeling as exhausted by their weekend as she was. She certainly didn't fancy the long drive back! As they looked at another beautiful sea scape, she made a mental note to stop for some caffeine before setting off properly.

"I just love the water," Beth said, looking at a beautiful oil painting of the scene that was displayed right in front of them. "It's just so mesmerising. That's what clinched the deal with moving to Dartmouth, I think; feeling so at peace when I looked over that water, with the sun shining off it…"

"The sun doesn't always shine off it!" Caspian said, as they moved along, out of the way of another couple.

"You know what I mean," she said with a smile. "You must feel it too - you and your midnight swims!"

"There is something rather enticing about the open water, I guess," he said.

"You missed your swim last night…"

"The only nights I've missed since April are when I'm away, or when I'm with you," he said.

"I hope I'm worth it."

"I think you are."

They were quiet again for a few moments, where Beth delighted in the glow of his compliment. Whenever she was with him, she felt like she couldn't quite get her thoughts straight. Words came out of her mouth without her thinking, and when she finally got what she wanted to say organised in her mind, he'd throw a comment like that her way and send her back into a mush. How long, she mused as she looked at a familiar looking scene, could that dizzying feeling last?

"It's Dartmouth," Caspian pointed out. "It's just not the view you're used to seeing. I think that's from Greenway - but right at the top of the gardens."

She looked it at a moment longer before answering. "Oh yeah, I see what you mean. I'll have to go up there on my next lunch break! It really is stunning."

"You think you made the right decision then, moving to Dartmouth on a whim?"

Beth grinned broadly. "I really, truly do."

The pleasant weather they had basked in at the beginning of September unfortunately didn't last as Autumn rapidly descended. The walk up to the main house at Greenway no longer seemed quite so exciting when it left Beth windswept and sodden, and she vowed to buy a really good quality raincoat on her next pay day. Then there was the day when the winds were too high for the ferry to run, and so she had to drive the long way round, ending up stressed and late, although Tanya had been very understanding.

"It's the pitfalls of living somewhere so beautiful," she'd said, as Beth had rung out her hair and tried to make herself look presentable for the tour group waiting. "We're surrounded by this beautiful water, but sometimes nature turns and it's more of a curse!"

"I think I'm falling out of love with the water," Beth muttered, pasting on a smile as she went to greet the group.

Tanya laughed. "That'll change when the rain stops!"

The fact that it had been two weeks since she'd seen Caspian wasn't helping Beth's mood. After she'd dropped him off at his mum's that Sunday evening, with strict instructions to apologise for keeping him out later than agreed, she'd gone home and slept until her alarm had gone off for the fifth time on Monday morning. He'd rung that evening, and explained he was having to travel to New York, and would be gone for a couple of weeks at least. She had taken heart in the fact that he'd sounded as disappointed as she'd felt.

"New York, though, that'll be exciting."

"I wish I didn't have to be away so long."

Me, too - that's what Beth wanted to say, but she was worried about things getting too intense, too quickly. Well, more intense than they had already been.

"Besides," he continued. "We still haven't gone for that coffee - at your sister's café."

Beth rolled her eyes, even though he couldn't see her. "Not forgotten about that, eh?"

He laughed. "Not a chance."

"All right, all right. When you get back, our next date can be coffee in Totnes. Not quite sure how it'll live up to previous dates..."

But it had been nearly two weeks since that conversation, and the weather was horrible and Caspian was not yet back. They'd spoken on the phone almost every other night, and she'd spent her free weekends adding to her novel - to the point where she felt like she was almost finished with the first draft. But none of that quite made up for the fact that they hadn't been able to go on a date for two weeks. Nor the fact that she was a little concerned with how much time she spent missing him...

It was Saturday night, just after seven, and Beth had finished her dinner and was contemplating the last scene of her novel, when there was a knock at the door. She pushed her notebook aside, a little puzzled - whoever was at the door would have had to get past Sam down in the fish and chip shop, so it had to be someone she knew. Her heart raced a little as she hoped it would be Caspian...

She flung the door open and her heart sank a little, and she chided herself for getting her hopes up.

"Any chance you don't have plans tonight?" Sam asked, still wearing his apron.

Her eyebrows knitted together. "Depends why you're asking..."

He flashed her a smile. "No hot date, I'm afraid - but I'm snowed under downstairs. Apparently when it rains, people can't be bothered to cook. Or something like that. Any chance you could come and give me a hand? I'll pay you..."

She sighed, and rolled her eyes. "Not making it easy for me to say no, are you," she said. "Turning up on my doorstep."

"Sorry..." To give him credit, Sam looked sheepish.

"No, no, it's fine, I'm just in a bad mood. Give me five minutes to get out of my pyjamas - no, no dirty comments needed, thank you - and I'll be down."

Another grin. "Thanks Beth. You're a life saver."

She closed the door and headed to her bedroom to rummage around for something she didn't mind smelling of grease and fish. She supposed she didn't really have any other plans, other than her novel, and the mood she was in probably wouldn't give the final romantic scene quite the right tone.

The shop was indeed packed, and since Sam had abandoned it to come and beg her for help, they were behind on the orders. She washed her hands, threw on her apron, and got stuck into dishing up the chips.

Time flew past in a flurry of orders and before she knew it, the clock on the microwave was flashing nine and the stream of people had slowed to a trickle.

"I wonder what brought that many people here," she mused aloud as she washed up. "It's not even the holidays!"

"The desire for chips is an unpredictable thing," said Sam, in a voice that suggested he thought he was saying something deep. Beth laughed; Sam threw a tea towel at her.

"Hello, what can I get you?"

She focussed on the washing up, thinking she could get her money and get into a nice hot shower to get rid of the smell of fish and chips as soon as she was done, when the response made her turn.

"Um… I was actually hoping to see Beth, who lives upstairs - can I knock?"

"Beth!" Sam shouted, although she wasn't exactly far away. "Loverboy's here."

She emerged from behind the dishwasher, horribly aware of the mess she must look. Nevertheless, she grinned when she saw Caspian, wearing a long black coat and covered in a fine mist of rain, stood at the counter. She even resisted the urge to throw the tea towel back at Sam.

"I didn't know you were back!" she exclaimed, drying the soap suds off her hands.

"Only landed a couple of hours ago…" he answered. "I did try to ring…"

"Sorry, Sam roped me in to help out, I left my phone upstairs." On cue, Sam handed her a twenty pound note.

"Thanks, Beth - I can finish up. Appreciate you saving me!"

"No worries." She hung the apron on the hook and slipped out from behind the counter to the door that led to her flat. "Coming up?" she asked with a smile.

"If that's okay…" He seemed unusually unsure of himself, and so she took his hand and led him up the stairs without answering.

Once inside, he removed his wet coat, hanging it neatly on the back of the door.

"I'm sorry," Beth said, "I'm a mess and so's the flat, and I smell like I spent longer than two hours in that chip shop."

"You look wonderful," Caspian said, running a hand through his hair. "I missed you."

Beth beamed. "Thank you for lying. And I missed you too. But I can't kiss you like this. Let me jump in the shower, okay - make yourself at home." It was as she walked towards the door that she realised she was missing out on an opportunity. She turned to face him, grinning and hoping her messy hair and greasy clothes weren't too much of a turn off.

"Unless you want to join me?"

For the first time in a while, Beth felt like she had a proper night's sleep. When she woke the next day, with no alarm and nowhere she needed to be, she felt truly rested. She watched Caspian for a while, still fast asleep next to her, and resisted the urge to trail her fingers across his face. He'd obviously been working too hard in New York, for there were dark circles under his eyes that she didn't remember being there on their weekend away. Perhaps it was the lighting, she thought - back then they had been bathed in sunlight, whereas now the persistent rain definitely gave everything a greyish tinge.

She slipped out of bed to make a drink, and decided a quick brush of her teeth and hair wouldn't hurt. As she entered the bathroom, she grinned to see the mess of their clothes dumped hurriedly on the floor. Things had felt a little awkward when he'd turned up, which she presumed was due to the two weeks apart, not to mention the jet lag she assumed he was suffering from. But the shower had certainly cut through any awkwardness, and she felt a sense of relief that he was back from being so far away. She hadn't liked not being able to see him, and had struggled to ring him at the right time for both of their timezones.

He was still fast asleep when she re-entered the bedroom with a mug of tea and one of coffee for him, so she took the opportunity to fish out her notebook. That last scene felt very much more within her reach now...

It was done. She had filed for a divorce from the man who had wanted to divorce her for so long - possibly since he had said 'I do'. He would languish in prison for a long time. Murdering his own father was an act so cold, she felt as though she had never known him. Although they had found his accomplice; the woman he had been in love with all this time, the woman he should have married in the first place. If he had done, perhaps none of this mess would have happened.

It was an hour later when she finally put down the pen.

Her tea was half drunk, his coffee cold and untouched, and in the notebook in front of her was the first draft of her novel. Finished. She couldn't quite believe she'd actually done it; stuck at it long enough to get it done. She didn't know if it was complete rubbish, or whether anyone would actually read it, but she felt a huge sense of achievement in writing 'The End' and knowing that there was one more story in the world thanks to her.

Brimming with excitement and energy, she grabbed her phone and snapped a photo of the closed notebook before sending it to Lee. *I finished my book!! X*

She didn't know why, but she wanted to tell someone, and Lee had always been her cheerleader, even if she generally thought Beth was being a bit flighty or too spontaneous. She didn't have to wait long for an answer, and the *bing* from her phone made her grin - and Caspian stir.

Wow!! So proud of you. Can't wait to read it! My sister, the author. Xx

You around today for coffee? Beth text back quickly, remembering her promise to Caspian about their next date.

I'm working in the café 'til 4, if that works? X

Perfect, Beth replied. *Someone I want you to meet! X*

Lee responded with a string of emojis to show she was both shocked and excited, and Beth put her phone down as Caspian's eyes flicked open.

"I didn't mean to wake you," she said, sat cross-legged on the end of the bed. "Although I hope your mum's not expecting you for lunch…"

"Is it that late already?" he asked, looking a little sheepish.

"Twelve, or there abouts."

"Is it awful if I told her I was back tonight so that I could spend more time with you?"

Beth felt her heart melt a little. "Doesn't sound awful to me." She leant across the bed to press a kiss to his lips, and felt his unshaven jaw against her delicate skin. "But I may be biased."

"It's not even like she'd have a problem with me saying I couldn't go for lunch," he admitted. "But I'd feel guilty. And to be honest, I got in the car at the airport and drove straight here. I didn't really think about it. Does that sound crazy?"

She shook her head, and then laughed. "Well, no more crazy than this whole thing has already been," she said. "I think we're just not very good at taking things slow."

"And you know," he said, sipping the coffee on the bedside table and then grimacing at how cold it was. "Previously I have had a girlfriend tell me I took things so slowly I might as well be going backwards."

"Mustn't have been the right girl," Beth said.

Caspian smiled. "I think you're right. Now, any chance of a hot coffee? I've got a killer case of jetlag, not to mention how late I was kept up last night…"

"Cheeky! It was hot when I made it, but someone slept in. Besides, I've had a very productive morning."

"Oh?"

Beth couldn't contain her grin. "I finished the first draft of my novel!"

"That's amazing!" He got out of bed and bent to kiss her, not bothered by his state of undress. "I can read it now then? You did promise!"

"It's only a first draft. I need to edit it first - and it needs typing. Which means I need to get a laptop!"

"I've got a spare you can have, if you want?" Caspian immediately offered, grabbing her pink dressing gown and appraising it, before wrapping it around himself, readying to search for coffee. "It's just sat around at mine."

"Really? That'd be great." She smiled, following him to the kitchen. "And in return, I'll follow through on a different promise. How does coffee at my sister's café sound?"

CHAPTER
TWENTY-FIVE

The roads were quiet on their drive to Totnes. They took Beth's car, as Cas still looked a bit tired to be driving. It seemed the rain had finally taken a pause for breath.

"Did you have a good time, then?" Beth asked, over-taking a cyclist who was looking drenched by the earlier downpour. "In New York, New York?"

"It was hectic," Caspian said, and Beth noted he was managing to keep himself from holding on to the handle above the door. "Meetings, dinners, new clients - the company's expanding, so I was working pretty much every hour I was there. No time to get over the jet lag at either end…"

"And tomorrow?" she asked, risking a quick glance at him before turning her eyes back to the road. "Do you have to travel again?"

He shook his head, but it was a moment before he answered, and there was a hesitancy in his voice that she didn't quite understand. "No, I can work from home for at least the next couple of weeks, maybe as much as a month."

Beth smiled broadly. "Lots of opportunities for amazing dates then, hey?"

They parked in a small car park just off from Totnes high street, and wandered through the quiet streets towards Lee's café. When Beth had previously been here the town was bustling, but it seemed the less than clement weather, combined with the fact that many of the small, independent shops seemed to be closed on Sundays, left the town quieter than usual. The chairs and tables outside the café were, unsurprisingly, empty, but Beth could see through the slightly misted windows that several tables were busy inside.

"There it is," she gestured, as they came to the door and paused.

Cas looked up at the sign; "Carol's café?" He glanced at Beth. "Who's Carol?"

"Our gran," Beth replied. "She passed away when we were young, but Lee wanted to name the café after her."

"That's nice."

The heavens opened once more, and they hurried inside, the chime of a bell announcing their arrival.

Her sister stood behind the counter, wearing a cupcake-covered apron and with her blonde hair scraped up into a bun. She was cheerily chatting with an older lady who Beth was sure she'd seen here before when visiting. As soon as she saw Beth, however, she made her excuses and hurried over to them.

"Beth! We live closer than we ever have done and I still barely see you," she said, giving her a hug. "I thought the promise of home-cooked food would have tempted you more often."

Although Beth enjoyed James' excellent home-cooked cuisine, she had avoided her sister's house the last couple of weeks. With Caspian away, she hadn't felt like she'd been great company - and she hadn't wanted to discuss the fact that a guy she was casually dating being away had put her in such a bad mood.

"Lee, this is Caspian," she said, meeting her sister's eye with a behave-yourself-or-else look. "Caspian, my sister Lee."

Cas held out his hand to shake hers. "Lovely to meet you," he said. "I've heard a lot about you!"

"She's been quite secretive about you," Lee said with a wink. "Although I hear you like to swim..."

Beth blushed and pushed her sister none too gently towards a table.

"This is a lovely café," Caspian said. "I used to come to Totnes for the markets all the time with my mum, but it's ages since we've been. I'll have to remind her."

"You're local then?" Lee asked, taking a seat at the table with them after checking that her co-worker, a young woman with blue hair and a lip-ring, was all right serving.

"Lived in Strete all my life," Caspian said.

"How lovely," Lee said. "I wish we'd grown up by the sea!"

"I think you get a bit complacent about it, when you see it all the time," Caspian said with a shrug. "Beth has made me realise how lucky I am!"

Lee smiled. "You know, my husband says exactly the same thing. Always takes the mickey out of me when I take my shoes off to feel the sand - no matter what the weather!"

"Can we get a drink?" Beth asked, interrupting her sister with a poke.

With a good-natured roll of her eyes to her little sister, Lee took their orders and returned with three steaming mugs. "If I didn't know better, I'd say my little sister wants to keep you all for herself," Lee said, ignoring Beth's blush and glare.

"I've got something I need to talk to you about," Cas said, when Lee had left them to go back to the counter after a sudden flurry of customers had come in, presumably to shelter from the rain.

"You met the love of your life in New York and are moving there?" Beth said, unsure why she was even joking about such a thing. Short relationship or not, she knew that would break her heart.

He shook his head with a gentle smile. "No, I promise that did not happen. But..." Beth felt her heart pounding as if it were going to break free of her chest. She felt tense at what words were about to come from his mouth; he seemed nervous. What the hell would he be nervous about telling her?

"Cas?" she prompted, when the silence got too much. She felt like the whole café was silent, when in fact it was buzzing with noise all around them.

"I've been offered a promotion. Heading up a new division of the company."

"Wow, Caspian, that's brilliant! Congratulations."

He smiled, but she didn't feel that rush of warmth that she usually did. That smile did not feel genuine; did not make his eyes shine or her skin tingle.

"It's in Edinburgh."

Beth felt her face fall; there was nothing she could do to stop it.

"Oh."

They were both quiet for a few minutes. Beth wrapped her hands round the mug, trying to find some words, and Caspian didn't push her.

"That's still really great, Caspian," she finally said, attempting to paste a smile on her face. "Running a whole new division, they must really trust you."

"I haven't decided if I'm going to take it yet," he said, sipping the end of his frothy coffee and swirling the dregs round the cup.

"No?" Beth felt some hope in her heart that she knew

she shouldn't be feeling.

"I've always lived here," he said, struggling to meet her eye. "My mum's here." He paused, and then there was a flash of his brown eyes meeting hers. "You're here."

She sucked in her breath at that; she hadn't been expecting him to be so candid. She took a deep breath, knowing what she needed to say, knowing what she should say, but finding the words painful to express. "We've only been on four dates, Cas," she said with a sad smile. "You shouldn't make a life-changing decision based on me."

It hurt, it physically hurt, when his eyes met hers again. She wanted to shout at him to stay, to of course make the decision based on her, that she wanted to see where this went and what amazing things lay ahead for them, that they needed to give those earth shattering fireworks a chance...

But she knew that wasn't fair.

She wasn't expecting to see the hurt bubbling up in his eyes.

She wasn't expecting to have to fight back tears.

"We should get going," she said, when he didn't respond, and he nodded.

She knew Lee could tell something was wrong, but to give her credit, she didn't comment. Beth was sure she'd get a phone call or at least a text later, but for now she just needed to leave. Just needed to escape the hell her mind had somehow become in the last few minutes.

How could everything have been so perfect, and now be so disastrous?

CHAPTER TWENTY-SIX

The drive back was quiet and awkward. They were almost back in Dartmouth when Caspian finally spoke. His voice cracked slightly, and whether it was through emotion or just a lack of use in the last twenty minutes, Beth wasn't sure.

"You think I should take it, then?"

Beth took a deep breath before she answered, in an attempt to control her emotions. "I'm not saying that." She didn't let the words slip out that she thought might sway him: *I don't want you to go.* "I just think you need to think about it. It does sound like an amazing opportunity."

"It does," he agreed, and the words felt like the knife was twisting. This was all going to end, she could tell; something which had more promise than any relationship she had ever been in, and it was going to be ruined by geography.

He didn't come up to the flat when they got back, but

instead fumbled around for his keys as they said goodbye. A kiss on the cheek, but even that felt forced, and then he was driving into the distance. Of course, he'd promised he'd see his mum, but that didn't make it any less painful.

Beth ducked behind customers as she entered the chip shop, avoiding Sam's eye, and slipped up the stairs to her flat. Her bedroom - where they had both happily lain only a few hours earlier, where she had felt so euphoric over finishing the first draft of her novel - made her feel too miserable, so she grabbed the duvet, curled up under it on the sofa and let the tears she'd been fighting finally fall.

Four days passed without a word from Caspian, although, if she were being charitable, she could acknowledge that she had not contacted him either. She travelled to work, took round tour groups, ate her lunch alone and came home, feeling the same sense of misery from when she woke up to when she fell asleep. She dodged a couple of phone calls from her sister, knowing she couldn't be on the phone without crying, and not wanting to show her sister how much this had meant to her - instead firing off some faux-cheery texts about being busy whenever she called.

Her novel sat untouched on the bedside table.

Then, on Thursday, at the end of a long day and a wet journey home, her phone beeped. She took a deep breath, steeling herself for another concerned messaged from Lee, and was surprised to see the name that popped up on the screen.

Caspian

She paused, then clicked to open it.

Are you free Sunday? Come round to mine, you can get that laptop, have lunch with me and my mum. Please? Cas x

The tone puzzled her. Were they even speaking? She was confused as to how they had left things the previous weekend, confused whether it was all over or whether there was still something left to save. But if he were moving to Edinburgh, was there any point?

Are you sure you want me to? X

The reply was almost instant: *Yes. Please come. I miss you. X*

She spent the next forty-eight hours debating whether or not she was going to go. Wouldn't it be awkward, having lunch with him and his mum when things between them were so up in the air? But then he had asked her to go. Maybe he had something he wanted to say... maybe there was some obvious way forward she was overlooking. She knew that didn't want things to be over between them; knew that there was a strong attraction there that she hadn't ever felt with anybody else. But there were the facts to consider: this was just the beginning of a relationship. It was not something well-established, not something where they'd told each other they were in love, not even where they referred to each other as boyfriend or girlfriend. It was the deliciously exciting beginning - but major life choices, she told herself over and over again, should not made based on four dates.

Beth hadn't even decided on Sunday morning whether she would be going or not, but by half eleven somehow found herself dressed in a blue dress and leggings, with her hair neatly put up and a bottle of wine in hand. She didn't know whether wine was even appropriate for Sunday lunch, but she felt odd turning up empty handed, so the bottle of wine was coming.

When she got in the car at quarter to twelve, she accepted her going had been inevitable; there was no way she could turn down a chance to see him, let alone a plea to come.

The drive was quick and she barely noticed the landmarks on the way, so caught up in her own thoughts was she. She wondered if she should discuss it all with someone - certainly not her mother, but Lee, perhaps, to help her get her head straight about the way she was feeling. It seemed like there had been a constant battle going on in her head since he had told of her his possible relocation, between what she knew was right and what she really wanted. Heart versus head, she supposed; she had always previously let her heart win, but that hadn't always worked out so fantastically.

As she parked in front of his house, she took a few minutes to steady her breath. She knew that seeing him would unravel her already scattered mind; it always did. He had a way of making her feel like she was melting away whenever he looked at her. She shook her head; imagining him before she saw him certainly would not help her to get herself together.

She was nervous, too, she realised as she knocked on the door; she hadn't been brought home to meet many mothers, hadn't wanted to meet them if truth be told, and yet she had wanted to meet Caspian's. Wanted to be liked by her...

He opened the door in a blue shirt and chinos, looking every bit as delicious as he always did. She smiled; she couldn't help it. Seeing him lifted her spirits instantly, and it was like the sun suddenly bursting from behind a cloud; she hadn't realised how grey it had really been until suddenly the sun shone.

"Hey," she said, handing him the bottle of wine before he even had a chance to speak. "I didn't want to come empty handed."

He smiled, and took it from her, leaning in to kiss her cheek. He lingered there for a moment or two and she could smell his aftershave, and a mintiness that she presumed was toothpaste. "I just wanted to see you," he said.

"I wanted to see you too," she said, her brain too frazzled to be anything but honest.

"Don't keep her on the doorstep, Caspian!" A voice came from inside the house, and Caspian rolled his eyes, grinning.

"Come in, Beth," he said, stepping aside and letting her pass him. She felt the warmth of his body through the shirt as she brushed against him, and felt a shiver go through her that had nothing to do with the autumnal weather.

"Mum, this is Beth," he said, as they entered the living

room. She was sat in the sofa, her greying hair pinned up in a bun, her eyes as warm as Beth remembered them being when they'd briefly met at Greenway, many months ago.

"Lovely to meet you, Mrs Blackwell," Beth said, holding out her hand.

"Oh, call me Mandy, Beth - and I have to say I'm very intrigued to meet the girl my Caspian can't stop talking about!"

Beth blushed, and she had a feeling she wasn't the only one. "I'll just, uh, check the meat," Caspian said, clearing his throat. "Drink, Beth?"

"Um, I'll have a glass of water, please," she said, feeling more nervous than she felt the situation really warranted.

"Well I'll have a glass of wine," Mandy said, patting the sofa for Beth to come and join her. "Beth?"

"Oh, go on then," she said with a flash of a smile. "But only a small one, I'll need to drive later." She was assuming she would not be staying over at Caspian's; for one, his mother was there, and secondly, she had no idea how the land lay with them.

"Now, tell me about yourself," Mandy said with a broad smile. "Caspian just hints at things but never actually gives me much information, for all he spends his time distracted by you. You're writing a novel, I hear?"

Beth was surprised that that was the piece of information Mandy knew. She supposed it was not the first thing she would tell somebody, but she was flattered Caspian had thought it important enough to mention.

"Yes, a murder mystery," she said, feeling a little more at ease in Mandy's company. "But I spend most of my time working over at Greenway."

"Ah, Greenway, I went there for the first time earlier this year - oh, that'll be why you look familiar!" she said. "I was sure I recognised you, but of course Caspian had said you weren't a local, so I wasn't sure how I knew your face!" Caspian reappeared at that point with three glasses of wine carefully balanced in his hands. "Caspian, would you believe Beth and I have met before? I can't believe you didn't realise, she was the guide that day at Greenway!"

Beth avoided Caspian's face and willed her cheeks not to redden. They had, of course, spoken that day at Greenway - and if she remembered correctly, it was for Caspian to tell her he still had her bra from their late night swimming session...

"How strange!" Caspian said, and Beth almost laughed at his acting. "What a coincidence."

"And you moved here recently, is that right?"

Beth took a sip of her wine as Caspian sat down on the armchair opposite. She tried not to be distracted by how well that shirt fit his chest, how he had left the top two buttons undone...

She filled Mandy in on her sudden move to Dartmouth, as well as her sister's, and by the time lunch was served she found her nerves had eased completely - possibly helped by the glass of wine.

It had been a while since Beth had eaten a proper Sunday roast - since the one James had cooked her, she supposed - and she tucked in to the delicious feast, listening to Caspian and his mum talk for a while without joining in, except to compliment his cooking. Somehow both she and her sister had grown up without any real cooking skills to speak of, and she was always impressed at anyone who could cook a proper meal.

"Mum taught me," Caspian said with a smile when she mentioned it. "It's not as good as her roast, of course, but I like to have a go. We quite often go out for lunch, but I fancied cooking today."

"He's modest," Mandy said. "He's always been a good cook - helped me for years as a kid before insisting on doing it himself most nights once he was a teenager!"

Beth laughed. "I can imagine him doing that!"

"Once Caspian decides he's doing something... well, there's no stopping him. Look at his job! Constantly rising through the ranks, even though he's one of the youngest in his team." She was clearly proud of her son; Beth could tell by the look in her eyes, as well as her glowing words. She wasn't sure if Mandy knew about the promotion yet - surely this would have been the time to mention it if she did? - but the topic just made Beth feel sad, and so she didn't bring it up. She had almost forgotten about it all, sitting here, having lunch with Caspian and his mum.

"You must be very proud."

"Very," Mandy said in a loud whisper. "But don't tell him that - he'll get a big head!"

After pudding - a homemade crumble that Mandy had brought with her, which was, of course, delicious too - Mandy made her excuses.

"Shall I drive you back?" Caspian asked, glancing out of the window.

"No, it's dry, and I fancy a walk after all that food. I'll be fine, thanks love." She put on a long black coat, and reached out a hand to take Beth's. "It was lovely to meet you, dear. Don't be a stranger, okay? Anyone who can make my Caspian smile must be a special person."

She thought she might well up at that, so Beth didn't answer; instead she tried to smile, and raised her hand to wave goodbye.

"I should make a move too," she said, as Caspian opened the door for his mum.

"No, stay, I need to show you how to set that laptop up," he insisted quickly. She was pretty sure she could set a laptop up perfectly well on her own, but she didn't push it, and left her coat hanging on the hook where Mandy's had been. She gave them a moment to say goodbye, hovering a little awkwardly in the living room doorway.

The door clicked closed and he turned to face her, and for a moment they stood there, eyes locked, words unspoken, in the greyish light from the doorway.

When they finally spoke, it was at exactly the same time.

"I'm sorry if-"

"I didn't want-"

Caspian grinned, and led her into the living room. "How about another glass of wine?"

"I won't be able to drive..."

"Then stay."

"Okay." She seemed incapable of disagreeing with him and, besides, she wanted to stay.

"I didn't like how we left things, the other day," he said, once they were both sat on the sofa with a much larger glass of wine each.

"Me neither," Beth said softly. She felt like she needed to guard her emotions, but felt wholly incapable of doing so.

"They only made the offer on the last day I was in New York," he said, stroking his fingers backwards and forwards over the palm of her hand, which was resting open on one of the sofa cushions. "I was still processing it when I spoke to you. I probably should have waited... but I wanted to see you." He smiled; "Beth, I always want to see you."

She swallowed, knowing him leaving would hurt even more if she let herself get in deeper, but not wanting to extricate herself. The words were beautiful as they washed over her like a warm breeze.

"We need to be honest," he said, when she didn't reply. "I need to be honest. Beth, we may have only been on four dates, but I know there's something between us. I want to do the whole dating thing - I want you to be my girlfriend, I want to spend lazy weekends in bed with you, I want to meet your family and support your dreams and-" he paused for breath. "I have never felt like this before. I have never wanted a relationship to work out more. I need you to know that."

Beth felt like she was holding her breath the whole time he spoke, waiting for the 'but'. There had to be one, right? Such a perfect, handsome, funny, clever man could not be saying all these things to her so soon - all these things that she was feeling too?

"Oh, Caspian," she said.

"But..."

And there it was. She stopped herself saying anymore; she knew it was coming. Things were never as perfect as they seemed.

"But I have to take this job, Beth. You were right; it's an amazing opportunity, and I've worked for it my whole life. I've got to do this."

Beth gulped, and took a large swig of her wine. "I get that," she said softly.

"So come with me."

"What?" She couldn't truly believe he had just said that; Caspian, the mystery, the man who seemed to want everything so perfectly ordered...

"You heard me. Move to Edinburgh with me."

"You're crazy!" Beth exclaimed, her mouth wide with shock, her wine glass frozen in mid-air as she tried to process his words.

"Crazy about you, Elizabeth Davis. I have never, ever done anything so spontaneous in my whole life. I don't want this to end, but I have to go to Edinburgh. You can write there - it's the city of Harry Potter! We can make a go of this. Beth, please, at least think about it?"

She felt dazed, and for a few moments said nothing.

"Just don't say no right away," Caspian pleaded, and then his lips were on hers and all rational thinking, all logic, all protests to his sudden declarations went out the window, and she gave herself over to Caspian's arms, and to the fireworks...

CHAPTER TWENTY-SEVEN

Beth barely slept that night. Even when Caspian slept next to her, she lay awake, mulling over his crazy request. How on earth could she up and move her life to another country? Hours away, no-one she knew anywhere close... She knew she seemed spontaneous, but moving an hour or so down to Dartmouth was absolutely nothing compared to this. And what about her job? And her sister?

These questions plagued her throughout the fitful night. Did he realise what he was asking? What would they do, live together? But what if she couldn't get a job? She didn't want to be a financial burden on him; that was a surefire way to end the relationship, she was positive. That was why you didn't make life decisions based on only a few dates; no matter the potential, all those stresses and strains could surely destroy a good thing.

Away from the practicalities, her thoughts turned to the idea of living in Edinburgh. She'd never been; but it looked wonderfully romantic in pictures and films. But it was a city, and she'd found such peace here in Dartmouth, with a slightly slower pace of life and a job she truly enjoyed. No, it wasn't some big career, but for now it made her happy, and let her pursue her writing hobby. Perhaps, one day, she dreamed, she could do something with her writing - but for now, this was a lot closer to reality. She loved living near her sister, seeing her niece grow up...

And then she thought about not moving to Edinburgh. Not seeing Caspian; not living that beautiful image he'd painted with his words the night before. Doing long distance and seeing each other once in a blue moon - or, even worse, ending their relationship all together. That hurt to even think of. She hadn't admitted as much to Caspian, but she wanted to be his girlfriend. Wanted to wake up next to him, wanted to see whether this could be real, true... love. She wasn't sure she'd ever really been in love, but if anyone was going to steal her heart, she thought it would be Caspian.

When he awoke the next morning to an early alarm, her eyes were wide open. Dark circles ringed them, and tears threatened to spill from them.

Caspian grimaced. "You're going to say no, aren't you." It wasn't even a question.

A lone tear fell from Beth's eye, despite her attempts to stop it. "I'm sorry, Caspian." Her voice was hoarse, and she felt a sharp pain in her ribs at even saying the words. "I can't up and move to a city, to Edinburgh. I just can't."

"I thought..." He didn't seem able to finish the sentence, and Beth swiped a hand across her eyes to wipe away the tears that were clouding her vision.

"I want to be your girlfriend. I don't want this to end... we could do long distance? I understand that you have to take this job... please understand that I can't just move there."

She was sure she saw emotions fluttering behind his brown eyes, but then they were gone, and the cold, hard exterior of the Caspian she had met on the beach had replaced them.

"It wouldn't work," he said, not mincing his words, and each felt like a knife. "Like you said: we've only been on four dates. How could we survive a long distance relationship? I know married couples who haven't coped with that kind of distance."

"But you'll be back to see your mum, surely," she said. "We could try…" She hated the begging tone of her voice, but she wasn't ready to give up on the possibility of *something* between them still.

Caspian shook his head.

He slipped out of bed towards the bathroom, and Beth waited until she heard the shower turn on before she began to get dressed, and let the tears fall furiously from her eyes. She needed to get out before he was out, she knew that; she couldn't meet that cold look of his again. Her heart was already shattered enough. When she'd finally found every item belonging to her, including a shoe that had ended up hidden behind a door somehow, she tried to slip out unnoticed.

"Beth, wait-"

She heard his voice and turned, hope rearing its ugly head, even though she wasn't sure what solution there even was to hope for.

"Don't forget that laptop. It's on the coffee table."

Her heart sank.

"I don't want it." Her tone was more bitter than the gesture probably deserved, but she couldn't help herself; not when he was hurting her so thoroughly.

"Please," he said, towel wrapped around his waist, hand mussing his hair more often than she thought necessary. "I want you to have it."

She turned on her heel, not saying a word, and at the last moment stopped to grab the laptop. She needed it, and there was no use cutting her nose off to spite her face.

In the car, with the door hastily shut and locked, she lay her head on the steering wheel and sobbed until she could cry no more tears.

She didn't allow herself to feel any hope when there was a knock on her door that evening. It had been a long and tough day at work, with too many lies needing to be told about 'allergies' or 'a bit of a cold' to explain her appearance. She'd breathed a loud sigh of relief as the last tour had finished and it was time to go home. Tanya had even caught her on the way out and told her to call in sick the next day, if she still felt bad. So when she finally got home, she skipped dinner, opened a bottle of wine and spent the evening on the sofa, doing everything she could not to think of Caspian and the crappy way everything had turned out.

The knock on the door had interrupted this difficult task, and when she opened it up she was surprised to see her sister stood there, a concerned look on her face and a bottle of wine in her hand.

"Lee," Beth said, fully aware of how awful she must look. "What are you doing here?"

Lee walked in without being invited, and looked her sister up and down. "I was worried. You were weird last week when I saw you, you've been dodging my calls and sending me these fake happy messages." She paused. "And to be totally truthful - and not to sound as harsh as our mother or anything - you look like crap."

"Thanks." Beth slumped back onto the sofa, not even bothering to argue it.

"Beth, what's the matter?" Lee's voice was full of concern, and it made the tears start flowing from Beth's eyes. She felt like a tap that it was impossible to turn off.

"Caspian and I... it's not going to work."

"Beth, I've never seen you like this before over a guy. What happened? What did he do?"

She drained her glass of wine, and without being asked, Lee unscrewed the lid of her bottle and topped it up.

"You'd best get a glass," Beth said with a sniff, and as her sister poured out some more wine, she proceeded to tell her how royally everything had gone down the drain in the last week.

"Wow," Lee said, when she got to Caspian asking her to move to Edinburgh with him.

"I know."

"I mean, I know you're the flighty type - no offence-"

"Plenty taken," Beth muttered.

"Oh, you know what I mean. But to move your whole life to another city, another country, the opposite end of the UK - what was he thinking!"

"You moved here for James…"

"I'd already moved here," Lee said softly. "I stayed for James."

Beth hiccupped, a result of wine combined with too many tears and not enough food. "Do you think I'm making a mistake?"

"I think you're being sensible," Lee said, and although to Lee it sounded like a compliment, Beth wasn't quite so sure.

"I think I could have loved him," Beth admitted, and then her tears started all over again Lee pulled her into her arms for a hug, and Beth stayed there for a long time, wishing she was as convinced as Lee that her decision was the right one.

She must have fallen asleep there, because the next thing she knew it was pitch black outside, and there was a blanket over her. She squinted around to see if she could see the time on the oven, although the alcohol seemed to have affected her vision somewhat, and saw a sandwich on the counter. 12.34am flashed on the oven. She groaned; work was going to be tough the next day.

She nearly jumped out of her skin when a figure exited the bathroom, and it took her a second or two to realise it was her sister.

"Lee, what are you still doing here!" Beth groaned, sitting up and feeling her head spin. "What about Holly?"

"James is perfectly capable of having a sleepless night having to take care of her on his own," Lee said with a smile. "And I wasn't just going to leave you, was I."

"You should have done," she said, as Lee brought the sandwich and a glass of water over to the coffee table. "I'm not exactly the best company."

"No, but you're my sister. And I was a bit worried you might have given yourself alcohol poisoning..."

Beth gave her sister a light shove. "I just hadn't eaten. I can handle a bit of wine with my heartbreak, thank you very much." She forced down a few bites of the sandwich, knowing she really needed to line her stomach.

"It's only cheese, I'm afraid - all you had in. You need some more food in the fridge!"

"I've had other things on my mind, Shirley..."

Lee grimaced, but said nothing.

"Sorry," Beth said a moment later. "You're right. And thanks for staying."

Lee sat next to her and took her hand for a moment. "I'm really sorry Beth. You will meet the right guy, I promise you."

"What if he was the right guy?"

Lee considered her for a moment. "Then it will work out somehow. I really believe that."

"Just because you got your happy-ever-after."

Lee couldn't help but smile. "But I went through the heart-ache too, remember?" There had been a time when she was crying on Beth's sofa and downing the wine... a time when she thought things couldn't possibly work out.

"Why do you always have to be so wise?" Beth asked, swigging the glass of water as though she had been in a desert for several hours.

"It's the perk of being the big sister."

CHAPTER TWENTY-EIGHT

Although she had only really seen Caspian on weekends, somehow now she felt as though she had an abundance of time on her hands that had to be filled, in order to stop her mind from wandering onto more miserable topics. She presumed he had left for Edinburgh, although she hadn't heard anything from him, and she had told herself she shouldn't get hold of him. She couldn't move to Edinburgh; he wouldn't do long distance. Hearing his voice was not going to fix those two incompatibilities.

Lee had invited her to stay the following weekend, something she thought she would most probably do. As October drew to a close, Lee and James' wedding plans were ramping up, and that was the guise Lee had invited her over under - maid of honour duties. They both knew that wasn't the reason, but Beth was happy to pretend otherwise. On the weeknights, to stop herself wallowing, she forced herself to pull out the laptop Cas had loaned her, and night by night she painstakingly typed up and edited the handwritten draft of her novel. It gave her something to focus on, and she was always thankful when she look up at the clock and found the hours had slipped by, and it was time to slip into bed - although sleep never came easily, and people at work often commented on how tired she looked. She worked doubly hard at being enthusiastic with the tour groups after these comments; the season had wound down and, although they were keeping her on for now, she had no idea whether there would be enough shifts for her though the winter.

She was pleased to have the distraction to get her through the week, and by the time Friday arrived, she had almost typed out every word in her notebook, not to mention adding to several of the scenes. She didn't feel quite the same sense of achievement as she had done when she finished the first draft, but she put that down to post-Caspian funk she was in and persevered anyway.

When she woke early on Saturday morning, Beth headed straight to Lee's, a small overnight bag in the back of the car, along with the laptop, just in case she felt like more writing. The weather seemed a little clearer than it had the last couple of weeks, although the leaves of the trees were a burnt orange and Halloween, as well as Holly's first birthday, was fast-approaching. She felt a sense of relief when she arrived at Lee's; she felt she needed the company, as well as the noise and excitement of a toddler, to keep her mind distracted.

"I left Exeter because I felt like none of it had any meaning," Beth said, as they sat making a wedding to-do list at the kitchen table. Holly played happily at their feet in a small, portable ball pit, currently occupied, although neither were sure how long that would last. "My job, guys I went on dates with, spending evenings on my own in that little flat…" She sighed, and took a glug of her tea. "And now I feel like things *do* have meaning, and I'm bloody miserable."

Lee reached over and squeezed her sister's hand. "You will feel better, Beth. It'll just take time. You still love your flat, right? And your job, and the novel writing…"

Beth nodded. "I guess."

"Trust me. By the time we get to my wedding, you'll be on to the next guy."

Privately, Beth thought that unlikely, but she didn't want to bring her negativity to all of Lee's wedding planning.

"Come on then. Distract me."

They spent a pleasant few hours finalising details and tasting cake samples that had been sent over, with James popping in and out to steal some cake and keep Holly entertained.

"And now," Lee said, opening up her laptop and typing in a password. "The last of the big jobs - your maid of honour dress. Now, I've let Gina choose her own bridesmaid dress - you've met Gina, right?"

"Ever-changing hair colour?" Beth asked.

Lee laughed. "That's her. I didn't have a clue what to pick that she would like, so I told her to choose one in red and that I'd be happy about it. So it seemed to make sense to let you all choose your own."

Beth raised her eyebrows. "Miss plan-everything-to-a-

T giving up the decision making on bridesmaids' dresses? Now I've seen everything! For your first wedding I had to wear that hideous yellow concoction. I mean..." She paused, realising that she wasn't really thinking through the words coming from her mouth. "Sorry."

She didn't know if Lee would feel uncomfortable with the discussion of her first marriage, or be insulted by Beth's clear lack of love for the dress she'd been forced to wear, but once again her sister surprised her. She gave a shrug; "Well, the less said about that the better. Anyway, you can do the same - pick a dress in red. We're paying, of course, although that doesn't mean you can go crazy..."

"Ha, ha," Beth said sarcastically. "Like I would. I'm not choosing something without your approval though - it's your big day!"

"Well, get some ideas, then maybe we can drive to Plymouth tomorrow and try some on, hey? If we combine it with a trip to a soft play place, I'm sure Holly'll be happy enough."

It was about twenty minutes into scrolling through pages of red dresses when Lee got up to make another cup of tea. As the kettle boiled, she sat on the floor with Holly, throwing the little plastic balls in the air, much to Holly's delight.

"Do you think... do you think people will think this is a bit much?" she asked all of a sudden.

"What?" Beth had been distracted by the dresses, and had not really heard her sister's question.

"You know. Having a whole big wedding, a white dress,

when this is my second time down the aisle."

Beth looked away from the screen and focussed her eyes on her sister.

"Of course not! What makes you think that?"

"Just thinking about my last wedding, I guess. I thought that was it, one time only, and now I'm doing it all again. To be honest, I'd be happy with something much smaller, but I want James to have a big day to remember too. After all, he's not done this before."

"Lee," Beth said, unusually dispensing the advice rather than being on the receiving end of it. "Nate destroyed your marriage. He was a cheating scumbag-" She avoided using the expletives she felt he deserved, as little ears were definitely listening intently "-and he could have ruined your life. But you got back on your feet, got a whole new life and you're properly, truly happy. Do not let him ruin your fairytale wedding; you deserve it. You both do."

"Thanks, Beth," Lee said, getting up of the floor to finish making the tea. "You can be pretty wise yourself sometimes, you know."

Beth grinned. "You and James are all that gives me hope in it all working out. You know, true love, happily ever after. I've got to believe in you!"

"No pressure, eh!"

Beth stayed up late in the guest room that night, putting the finishing touches to the first draft of her novel.

Well, the second draft, she corrected herself; a lot of changes had been made as she'd transferred the text from her notebook to the screen.

She'd promised Caspian he could be the first to read it, but that didn't seem likely now. She sighed as she closed the lid; perhaps Lee would want to read it. Somehow, letting anyone other than Cas comment on it first felt wrong, and so perhaps it would be destined to languish on the laptop for a long time to come...

◆ ◆ ◆

"I am absolutely exhausted," Beth said dramatically as she threw herself down on the sofa, not bothering to take off her coat or put the down the many bags she was carrying. Lee carried a sleeping Holly, and flicked on the light switches as they walked in to illuminate the dark house. James was working late, and so the house had been empty most of the day; it felt cold and she looked forward to lighting the fire.

"Me too," Lee said, lying Holly down on the sofa next to Beth. "And now she's fallen asleep so late, I'll not have a hope of getting her down at bedtime! Still, a drive like that was bound to send her off to sleep."

"I don't think I've ever tried on so many dresses or pairs of shoes in my life!"

"Hmm," Lee said with a smile. "I'm not sure that's completely true. At least we found one though!" Not only had they found a dress for Beth for the wedding, as well as matching shoes and a clutch, they had also found dresses they both loved for the next time they went on a night out ("Although when that will be, with a one-year-old, God only knows," Lee had commented as they paid), some new clothes for Holly and a jumper that she thought would match James' blue eyes perfectly.

"Takeaway for dinner?" Lee asked, and Beth nodded. "It's awful, most nights James cooks, and then he's not here and I just get a takeaway!"

"You work two jobs and look after a toddler, you deserve it. Besides, you know neither of us is any good at cooking!"

"I'm trying to learn!" Lee said from the kitchen. "But, like you said, limited time. Chinese or Indian?"

Beth thought for a moment. "Indian!" she shouted back, and Lee reappeared with a takeaway menu.

"They're not online... it's old school phoning up and ordering! Pick what you want - I'm going to go and get Holly at least ready for bed. Since she had her dinner so early, she'll probably need a snack... the routine is definitely out the window today!"

She disappeared upstairs while Beth perused the menu, before hearing a call of "There's wine in the fridge!" Although Beth felt she had probably drunk more wine in recent weeks than was really prudent, it would be rude to refuse - and as she was off work again the next day (due to Greenway being closed for a private wedding that certainly did not need a tour guide), she didn't need to worry about getting home tonight, or having a hangover the next morning.

She poured large glasses of wine for both of them, knowing Lee wouldn't touch hers until James was home to be in charge of Holly, but feeling better about not drinking alone, and took a long sip of the cool, crisp white wine.

"Decided?" she asked, and Beth nodded.

"Prawn balti," she said. "And whatever rice and naan bread you want."

"I'll order something for James too, then when he gets in he can reheat it. Wife-to-be of the year, hey!"

"He's lucky to have you."

By the time James got home, Beth was a little giggly from a second glass of wine. Lee joined her then, and the three of them sat on the sofa, James hungrily tucking in to his reheated curry.

"When did you know you loved Lee, James?" she asked.

"Beth!" Lee exclaimed. "You don't just ask people things like that."

"He's not people. He'll be my brother-in-law in six weeks' time!"

James smiled. "If I say the first time I saw her, is that too soppy for you?"

"Yes," Beth said, suddenly feeling a little morose.

"Hey, I didn't mean to upset you!" It must have shown

on her face, then, although she was trying to look care-free.

"I'm fine," she said, knowing that the wine was no longer helping her mood.

"He's an idiot, if he can't see what a good thing he's got," James said, and although Beth didn't know how much of the situation he knew about, his words were kind.

"Maybe I didn't know what I had..." she mumbled, and when no-one jumped into the conversation, she found her mouth continuing to talk without any real thought. "He wanted to jump all in - I'm the one who didn't want to move my whole life to another city."

"Another country!" Lee added. "Beth, he shouldn't have asked you, shouldn't have put that pressure on you. And he should have given long distance a go."

"Is it possible," James asked, "- and please tell me if this is none of my business - that he was hurt by you saying no?"

Beth paused, trying to consider his words but finding her head a little fuzzy. What was it he'd told her on the beach? His greatest fear was being left heartbroken.

Had she hurt him?

"I'm hurt by him leaving," she mumbled, and Lee pulled her into a hug that she so desperately needed.

It wasn't much later when Beth made her excuses and

slipped into the bed in the spare room. Her head was spinning a little, and she had lost track of how many glasses of wine she had drunk; a second bottle must've been opened at some point. When sleep did not come easily, she pulled the laptop out of the drawer next to the bed for safekeeping (just in case Holly had made her way into the room), and opened it. There was a label on the left hand side, next to the track pad, and she ran her finger around the outside of it, reading the words over and over.

Caspian Blackwell
Caspian.Blackwell@mail.net

She didn't know how old the laptop was, whether it was even an email he still used, but without pausing to think it through, she opened up her emails and began to type.

Because I promised.

Beth

She attached the document with her novel and hit send, not giving herself a chance to change her mind, then closed it and shoved it back in the drawer as if it had never happened.

Knowing she was probably only opening herself up to more pain, she let sleep overcome her and dreamed fitful dreams until Holly's cries of 'mama!' woke her the next morning.

CHAPTER TWENTY-NINE

She tried not to check her emails; tried to pretend that she hadn't sent it to him. In a way, it was like she hadn't; there was no reply, no acknowledgment of it at all. She wondered if it were an old email address, or if he really was hurt, like James had said. Or maybe he just didn't care. Perhaps she was reading far too much into all of it.

It wasn't really a conscious decision, but for the next few weeks she didn't look at the notebook, or the laptop. She felt like it needed to be left for a bit; and if she were honest, she had no idea what to do with it next. Perhaps she would give it to Lee to read, but that could wait until the new year. The build up to Christmas was in full swing, and she focussed on little things in her day that she found enjoyable. Christmas lights strung through the trees at Greenway; the festive drinks Lee was serving at the café; watching Christmas films in her pyjamas at the weekends. One thing she was trying not to enjoy so frequently was wine; she had realised how commonplace a hangover was becoming, and although Christmas time wasn't exactly a traditional time for cutting back, she didn't have any social occasions she wanted to attend - besides her sister's wedding. She was trying not to contemplate the fact that she would have to witness such a beautiful display of love two days before Christmas completely alone.

Nothing like a wedding to make you feel sorry for your own lack of a love life.

Her hours had been reduced a little at Greenway, due to the fact that fewer people wanted to roam the gardens in the middle of winter, but Sam gave her a few shifts in the chip shop and so she could survive all right on her earnings. That was how she found herself sat in her pyjamas watching yet another soppy Christmas film on a Wednesday morning, when there was a knock on the door.

When she opened it, she was surprised to see the postman; he usually left her mail with the shop's downstairs, and she collected it when she remembered. It was almost always bills, anyway.

"Package for you to sign for," he said, handing her the electronic pad and then the flat, brown-paper parcel. It had 'fragile' stamped across it in red lettering, and Beth was intrigued; her bank balance hovered in the black, but she hadn't had enough to do any online shopping in a while. She'd already made excuses to her family in advance for the lack of Christmas presents they would be receiving - Holly would probably be the only one who got a proper gift.

Curiosity got the better of her, and as soon as she closed the door she ripped off the paper. The back of a frame came into view, and when she turned it over, her heart felt like it stopped. There, behind the glass, was the painting they had seen in the gallery in Newquay; Dartmouth viewed from the very top of the gardens at Greenway. She never had done the steep walk up there to look for herself, but she recognised it now, with its vivid blue water, and orange and red sky. And she knew there was only one person who could have sent it.

Tucked into the corner there was also a letter. Her hands shook as she opened the unmarked envelope, and two heavy sheets of paper slid out. One was typed, one handwritten, and it was that one she was drawn to first.

Dear Beth,

I bought this for you in Newquay. I wanted you to have it.

I loved your story, and showed it to a friend of mine who I do publicity for. He has a small press and is really interested. Please don't be angry - I wanted to share how amazing it was. I've enclosed his offer to work with you - please at least think about it. No pressure.

Caspian.

She had to sit down before she read the next piece of paper, and in truth she reread the first several times before unfolding the second. It was much more formal, and introduced the gentleman - Sean Johnson - and explained the royalties he could offer and the editor he worked with.

It was all too much to take in.

Communication from Caspian - the first in weeks.

Such a beautiful reminder of the most perfect weekend she had ever had.

And a real, down to earth offer to publish the book that

she'd scribbled in a notebook on her way to work, and in her lunch breaks.

She put the papers down, her hands still shaking a little, and made a cup of tea that she very much wished was wine.

◆ ◆ ◆

It was growing dark outside by the time she'd wrapped her head around everything that package had contained. She couldn't find it in herself to be annoyed at him for sharing her work without asking; somehow, she could tell he'd only done it for the right reasons. She was astounded anyone thought it was good enough to take any further; but the first decision she made was that yes, she would contact this Sean. After all, she'd talked about having meaning, talked about finding a career and a hobby that gave her more of a purpose - and this was surely a huge stepping stone to that. She'd be a fool to turn it down, even if it made her very nervous.

The painting she hung on her bedroom wall, knowing that every time she looked at it she would feel happy, even if it was tinged with sadness. She tried not to let her emotions about how things had turned out interfere with her memories of that perfect weekend in glorious Newquay.

The final issue wasn't so easy to deal with: whether she should contact Caspian. On one hand, she thought it would be extremely rude not to; on the other hand, she had been the one to start the communication - perhaps she should be the one to let in lie.

But on yet another hand, she really, really wanted to

speak to him.

Even if she knew it would hurt.

CHAPTER THIRTY

She made herself wait until the next day, but when she woke up early for work and saw the framed picture on the opposite wall, hung a little off centre, she couldn't help herself. It took her a moment to decide what to write; she went with the simple sentiment that she felt needed expressing.

Thank you.

The response came while she was in the shower, and it was only as she packed her lunch into her bag for work that she saw it.

You're welcome. I really enjoyed your book.

She didn't know what to reply to that, other than 'thank you', which seemed a little redundant, and so she forced herself to throw the phone in the bottom of her bag and leave it there.

The air was crisp but the sky blue, and she found her journey to work more enjoyable than it had been in recent weeks. The ferry had old-fashioned Christmas lights wrapped around any surface possible, and it made her smile as it pulled into the harbour.

"Morning!" John the fisherman called from his frequent spot on the bench overlooking the water. His coat was a heavier winter one, but he was still out in all weathers, despite his clearly advancing years.

"Morning!" she called back.

"Still writing that novel?"

"I finished," she said with a smile.

"When will I be seeing it in bookshops?" he asked with a smile of his own.

"One day soon, I hope! See you later!" She practically skipped onto the ferry, unsure what had put her in such a good mood, but embracing it none the less.

The tour groups were small that day but cheery, and Beth enjoyed taking them round the property, which had been decorated with the Christmas ornaments Agatha Christie herself had bought for her family, as well as greenery from the extensive gardens. Everybody seemed to be embracing the Christmas spirit, and when she returned them to the front desk at the end of the tour, she was pleased to hear several of them excitedly talking about everything they'd learnt.

"Oh, Beth, perfect timing," Tanya called over. "There's someone on the phone for you!"

Beth furrowed her brow slightly - no-one had ever phoned her at work. She didn't think she'd ever given the number to anybody, although she supposed it wouldn't be that hard to find online.

She picked it up and waited a second for Tanya to head back out to the front desk. "Hello?"

"Oh, hello, Beth. It's Mandy here, Caspian's mum."

"Oh. Hello, Mandy." Her heart was racing - had something happened? Mandy didn't sound perturbed, but why on earth would she be calling her at work?

"Sorry to call you at work, dear, but I didn't know how else to get in touch with you!"

"That's fine," Beth said. "Is... is everything okay?"

"Yes thank you. It's silly really, but I was hoping you could help me. I've had a Christmas tree delivered, and I told the young man I'd be fine getting it in the house by myself, but I don't seem to be able to get it through the doorway. I don't really have anyone else to ask, and I was wondering if there was any chance you could come round and give me a hand?"

It seemed a very strange request from a woman she had only met twice, but she was so pleasant and warm on the phone that Beth didn't feel she could refuse. Besides, it was all in the spirit of Christmas, wasn't it?

"Of course I can," she said. "I can come round after work, say five o'clock?"

"Perfect," she said. She reeled off her address for Beth to note down, before saying her goodbyes. Beth paused for a minute, wondering how she had ended up agreeing to help her ex-whatever's mother move a Christmas tree, before hurrying back to her next tour group.

It was slightly after five when she reached Mandy's house; it had taken her longer than planned to get home and collect her car, and then she'd taken a wrong turn on the winding roads through Strete and missed the house entirely. From the light streaming from the living room window, she could see the large fir tree propped against the house, and wondered why the delivery boy hadn't insisted on taking it inside. She only hoped she could manage it.

She knocked on the door and was welcomed in by Mandy, who had a fire roaring in her real fireplace.

"Oh, thank you for coming!"

"Sorry I'm late," Beth said. "Where shall I bring it in to, then?" she didn't remove her coat or gloves, knowing she'd need them out in the chilly wind.

"Just into the living room, please. I'll come and give you a hand, it's definitely too heavy for one person! I think I ordered one far too big, but I do love Christmas."

"You remind me of my sister!" Beth said as they headed out into the cold. "She can't get enough of Christmas!"

Between them they manhandled the tree through the door. Beth was a little worried they might have taken the top off it, but she supposed decorations could hide any bare patches. Getting it through the narrow living room door was even harder, but with a lot of grunting and pushing they eventually reached the designated corner, and Beth held it upright with some difficulty as Mandy screwed it in to the stand.

"Marvellous," she said, with a broad grin that reminded Beth of Caspian's smile. "I feel properly Christmassy now. Thank you for coming out of your way to help me. Let me get you a drink. Tea? Coffee?"

"I should get back…"

"Go on, one drink, please? I want to say thank you." Her eyes were kind when she met Beth's, and Beth found herself nodding.

"Okay. Tea please."

They sat in front of the fire for longer than Beth planned, and somehow Caspian was not mentioned. She was sure that was intentional, because had Mandy not known of their situation, surely she would have mentioned him at least once? He was the link between them, after all. Instead they talked about Christmas; Beth told her about her sister's Christmas wedding, and Mandy lamented that Beth had not had a chance to experience the Christmassy spirit around the area, other than in Dartmouth and at work.

"Oh, the Christmas market in Totnes is one not to miss," she said, and Beth smiled.

"My sister keeps going on about that, so I'm sure I'll make it there at some point!"

"And have you seen the driftwood Christmas tree down at the beach? It's beautiful strung with lights at night. I think one of the local hotels puts it together every year. Always slightly different, but brings that bit of festive magic to the seaside. You should definitely stop by and see it."

As she began to get hungry and heard the clock in the

hallway strike seven, she insisted she had to go. "Have a lovely Christmas," she said, leaning to kiss Mandy on the cheek.

"You too, dear. I hope to see you again, sometime."

She wasn't sure when that would happen, but she echoed the sentiment and hurried through the cold air to her car.

She had begun driving home when, on a whim, she decided to go and look at that driftwood Christmas tree by the beach. As much as she had enjoyed talking to Mandy, it had brought a touch of sadness to her day as she remembered the lunch they had shared and what she was missing out on. And Lee did always tell her that Christmas spirit made everything seem better. Granted, she had never been quite as obsessed with Christmas as her sister, but Lee did have a tendency to be right about most things.

Beth felt a shiver as she pulled up in the dark car park overlooking the beach. It was that same car park where she had gone for her reckless late night swim back in the summer; that same beach where she had met Caspian for the first time. Where she had kissed him...

She got out of the car and pulled her coat tightly around her body. It was so much colder here, exposed to the bitter wind from the sea. Just as Mandy had described it, there on the path leading to the beach was a tall tree made of driftwood at different angles. Multi-coloured lights - which she presumed were battery operated - were strung around it, just about bright enough to be reflected in the waves that lapped the beach. It had a rustic charm that made her feel a little warmer inside, and as she turned back to the warmth of her car, she was sure she had made the right decision in stopping off here on her way home.

And then...there he was.

She knew it was him, even in the darkness; she recognised the way he stood, his profile in the light of the moon and those Christmas tree lights. He stood not a metre from the tree, very still, looking out to sea, and she didn't think he had noticed her up in the car park. There were no other cars here; had he run, like he had in the summer?

Her feet moved without permission from her head, and as her boots crunched in the sand, he turned his head and she thought she saw a smile in the moonlight. She stood next to him, shaking a little, feeling a tension between them, feeling like there was some gap that could not be bridged.

"Not swimming tonight?" she finally said, and was rewarded with a laugh.

"I think it would give me a heart attack," he said. "So no, not tonight. You?"

She shook her head. "I never was as dedicated as you."

Silence.

"How's Edinburgh?" she finally asked, feeling like it was a silence that had to be filled.

He paused, and she didn't look at him as he answered. "There's no fireworks there."

She turned then to face him, needing to see his eyes, desperate to touch his skin - but holding herself back.

"I miss you," he said, and she felt like the coldness surround her was melting away.

"I miss you too," she answered. "I miss the fireworks."

He took a step towards her, and for a moment they stood on that beach, waves crashing behind them, a centimetre or so between them, and felt the emotions shimmering in the air around them. Then he moved his icy, gloveless hand to her face and stroked his thumb across her cheek.

"I've been a total idiot," he said, and she only realised she was crying when she felt the warm, salty tracks down her cold face.

"I still can't move to Edinburgh," she said, not wanting to break the spell between them but knowing she needed to make sure there were no misunderstandings.

"I know," he said. "We can do long distance. It's Christmas in what, ten days? I can be here for a couple of weeks then. We can give it a go…"

"I've always wanted to visit Edinburgh," Beth said with a watery smile.

"I just want to be with you," Caspian said. "However we can do it, that's all I want."

And then his lips were on hers and it was like the cold night air didn't exist. The fireworks fizzed through both of them, burning a trail of desire that Beth wasn't sure she'd ever be able to sate.

"Will you do one thing for me?" she asked, her breath slightly ragged.

"Anything."

"Be my date to my sister's wedding?"

He grinned. "With pleasure."

CHAPTER THIRTY-ONE

Epilogue

The day dawned bright but cold, with a frost on the ground but no clouds in the sky. It was beautiful weather for a Christmas wedding, and although there was no snow, Beth was pleased there was no rain as had previously been forecast. As had been the case for every day Caspian had been back in Dartmouth of the festive period, she woke up next to him and grinned. She didn't dwell on the fact that, come New Year, he would be back in Edinburgh, because they had a plan: she would go with him, for the Hogmanay celebrations in Edinburgh, and stay for a couple of weeks. Work had already granted her the time off - in fact, she thought they were a little pleased, as it was no secret that there were far fewer hours to go around in January. She could meet Sean, Caspian's publishing friend, who she had tentatively emailed an agreement to, and she could even begin work on a second novel.

They had a plan.

Yes, it was very long distance. Yes, it was going to be

tough. But they had both agreed to throw out the nonsense of 'only four dates'; they didn't want to be apart. And that was all that truly mattered.

"I'll meet you there?" she said, pressing a kiss to his lips and running her fingers across his unshaven jaw line. She was getting ready with her sister, and she was already in danger of being late.

"I'll meet you there. Dartington Hall, twelve o'clock," he recited.

"Don't be late!"

"When am I ever?" he asked. "I'm going to have a leisurely coffee, a hot shower, get into my suit and be there in plenty of time. You, on the other hand, need to hurry up so the bride isn't stressed!"

Beth grabbed her bag and turned back to face him as she reached the door. "Make sure you're not late, because you know otherwise, tradition would dictate I have to flirt with the best man - and as he is James's married brother, I'm not sure it would go down too well."

"I promise you I will not be late - and no best man or groomsman will be getting anywhere near you. Now go!"

She laughed all the way down the stairs.

The music began, and Beth squeezed her sister's hand. "Ready?"

"One hundred percent," Lee said with a smile, looking radiant in a soft white gown with a bright red trim.

They hugged and tried to avoid tears that had been threatening to spill over all day, and one at a time the bridesmaids made their way down the aisle, with Beth bringing up the rear. She caught Caspian's eye in the crowd and was very pleased with the look he gave her; she knew she had chosen the right dress. Red, of course, with a ribbon round the waist and a v-shaped neckline. The heels helped to make it sway as she walked, and she had sudden vision of herself walking down an aisle as a bride herself.

One day, she thought, it would be her wedding.

And it would be Caspian standing at the end of the aisle.

And they would most definitely end their reception with fireworks...

The story - and the wedding! - continues in the next book, 'The Best Christmas Ever'. mybook.to/bestchristmas. Read on for a sneek peak.

THE BEST CHRISTMAS EVER

Thirteen weeks until Christmas

Lee Davis had always been organised. As a child, she'd made lists to organise her dolls, made homework diaries well before she'd ever been assigned homework, and often reminded her mum and younger sister about appointments and plans. She loved to know what was going to happen and when - and that was possibly why everyone had been so shocked when, almost two years ago, she had started her life again in the rural town of Totnes, Devon.

Of course, there had been rather a shocking catalyst to that event, which had made her jump so far out of her comfort zone. Walking in on her husband, Nathan, sleeping with a blonde he'd met at work had finished their marriage, and made Shirley reconsider everything she'd ever known.

But despite a few spontaneous decisions - the trip to Totnes, buying a café, falling in love, having a baby - at heart, she still loved organising. And so when she had set out to plan her wedding to James, the gorgeous policeman who had stolen her heart and fathered her baby, she had set to it with a fresh notebook and a great deal of excitement.

And yet...

Somehow, everything seemed to be taking a lot longer than planned. She found herself putting off tasks that she should have completed, or debating decisions for far longer than they needed. Should she have a white dress? Was it ridiculous to have four bridesmaids the second time around? Who on earth would walk her down the aisle?

She had never expected planning the wedding to the love of her life to be so complicated.

"Do you need any help?" Beth, Lee's younger sister, asked one night over the phone.

"No, it's all fine," Lee lied. They had spent a long while discussing Beth's new love interest, who Lee couldn't wait to meet, and so it had taken quite a while for the conversation to come round to the wedding.

"Are you sure? I was expecting to be inundated with dress fittings and maid-of-honour duties by now; it's only three months to go! You definitely have got your dress?"

"Yes, yes, I told you when you were round that I had it!"

"Hmmm. Not sure I'll believe that 'til I see it."

"Well you won't be seeing it until the wedding day, so I guess I'll have to cope with your disbelief!" Privately, Lee wasn't too sure whether she was going to keep the dress. She'd fallen in love with it when she'd seen it in the little bridal shop round the corner from the café she owned in Totnes. She'd only gone in on a whim, with a rare bit of time without her almost one-year-old daughter Holly or her husband-to-be, and had certainly not expected to buy a dress in the first shop she'd looked in.

But there it had been; hanging towards the back of the shop, on sale and in Lee's size. That alone seemed like a sign. It was white satin, very simple, with a scooped neckline and the most beautiful red satin trim around the train. It was perfect - the red would fit her Christmas wedding theme, and when she tried it on, she knew she just had to have it. She told James she'd bought it, although of course he wasn't allowed to see it, and had let Beth and her mum know, when they'd asked - but it was hung in the back of her wardrobe, not to be seen by anyone until the big day.

It was about a week after she'd bought it that she'd started to have doubts. When she got it out of the wardrobe to take another look, she worried it was too much; too beautiful, too white, too exquisite to be a second wedding dress. Outside of the luxury of the shop, it seemed much more decadent, and she found worries creeping in that their guests might not feel she should be wearing something so beautiful.

These worries had not been voiced to anyone; she knew Beth would say she was being ridiculous. James would reassure her - but this was only his first wedding, and she didn't really like to discuss her first failed marriage more than she had to. She certainly didn't want him to feel guilty about their big day - and he deserved to have the big white wedding too.

So she took to sighing every time she looked at the dress - but not actually making any decisions either way about whether she would wear it.

"Lee? Are you even listening?" Her sister's voice on the other end of the line brought her back to reality.

"Sorry Beth. Yeah, I am, carry on..."

Available now on Amazon: mybook.to/bestchristmas

AFTERWORD

Thank you so much for reading 'Feeling the Fireworks'. I hope you enjoyed it and would love to hear from you in a review on Amazon or an email to rebeccapaulinyi@gmail.com!

Although there has been some artistic license used, most of the places in the novel are real and are places I have visited. If you get a chance to visit Greenway, especially on a sunny day, it's well worth a visit! When I was there I could very much imagine someone being inspired to write, and it definitely reignited a love of watching Poirot episodes!

To hear about new releases, see pictures of my daughter and dog and generally hear about my writing, you can sign up to my newsletter here: tiny.cc/paulinyi

You can read Lee and James' story in 'The Worst Christmas Ever?' (mybook.to/worstchristmas) and 'Lawyers and Lattes' (mybook.to/lawyersandlattes), and you'll be able to see more of Lee's wedding in the upcoming 'The Best Christmas Ever' (mybook.to/bestchristmas)! To read more of Beth and Caspian's story, you can now buy 'Trouble in Tartan' (mybook.to/troubleintartan), and the series will be completed by 'Summer of Sunshine' (mybook.to/summerofsunshine)!

Happy reading!

BOOKS IN THIS SERIES

Finding herself and flirting with the handsome local police officer might just make this the best Christmas ever.

Lawyers And Lattes

A new home, a new man, and a new career are all great - but do they always lead to happily-ever-after?

Shirley 'Lee' Jones has made some spontaneous and sometimes questionable decisions since the breakup of her marriage, but deciding to remain in the quirky town of Totnes has got to be the biggest decision so far. Now Lee has a new business, gorgeous man, and friends keeping life interesting. But when questions of law crop up in her life again, she finds herself yearning for the career and the life plan she gave up when she left everything behind.

And when unexpected news tests her relationship, her resolve, and everything tying her to her life, Lee must decide between the person she is and the person she wants to become.

Sometimes decisions about life, law, and love all reside in grey areas. Will Lee's newfound happiness in Devon be short-lived? Or could her new life give her the chance to have everything she's ever wanted?

Feeling The Fireworks

Can Beth rekindle her passion for life and love in picturesque Dartmouth?

When Beth Davis made a whirlwind decision to move to picturesque Dartmouth to shake up her repetitive life, the last thing she expected to find was a passion in life - or a man who could make her feel fireworks.

A change in home and job seems like exactly what Beth needs to blow away the cobwebs that have been forming around her dead-end job. With little money to her name and no real plan, Beth needs to make things work, fast - without relying on her big sister Lee to bail her out.

When she meets the handsome, mysterious Caspian in a daring late-night swim, she instantly feels fireworks that she had long forgotten. Can Dartmouth - and Caspian - re-awaken her passion for life and love?

'Feeling the Fireworks' is Book 3 in the South West Series but can be read as a standalone novel. Fall in love with Devon today!

The Best Christmas Ever

A Devon wedding with the magic of Christmas and a dose of small town charm - and the potential for a lot of family drama.

Lee Davis is about to marry the man of her dreams - and at her favourite time of year. But she's finding it hard to feel the magic of Christmas or the excitement about her wedding as a face from her past reappears and worries about her second time down the aisle surface.

James Knight thought he had everything - the woman

he was destined to be with, an adorable daughter and a happy life in the countryside. But with his wife-to-be seeming more and more distant, is he doomed to be jilted at the alter again?

Beth Davis is pretty sure she's lost her heart to handsome, brooding Caspian - but he's moved away to Edinburgh, and their fiery romance seems to have been stopped before it had truly started.

Caspian Blackwell wants to be excited about his promotion and moving to an vibrant new city - but his heart is very much back in Dartmouth.

Can a festive Devon wedding make this the Best Christmas Ever?

Trouble In Tartan

Beth Davis didn't plan on falling in love when she moved to Dartmouth - she just wanted to feel some fireworks. The problem is, she's pretty sure that is exactly what is happening - but the object of her affections is living 600 miles away in Edinburgh. As she tries to start a career as an author, downs a few too many glasses of wine and attempts to make ends meet, keeping a long-distance relationship alive proves more and more challenging.

Caspian Blackwell has never let his heart make big decisions - but he's sorely tempted when the distance between them begins to cause problems in his relationship with Beth. When he decides he wants all or nothing, can he really put this new relationship before his career? Or will he end up exactly where he always feared he would: heartbroken?

A tale of love, longing and a relationship stretched between coastal England and Scotland.

Summer Of Sunshine

A summer holiday can wash up a whole host of family dramas...

Lee Knight wants to relax on a summer holiday away with her husband, sister and brother-in-law. But her desire for another baby is not making it easy to unwind.

James Knight hates to see his wife upset, and hopes a trip away will make her troubles lessen. But with concerns about his father's health, he's finding it hard to be there for her as much as she really needs.

Beth Blackwell is sick to death of everyone asking her two questions: when is her next book coming out, and when is she going to have a baby. The first is proving more difficult than she expected, and the second - well, she's not sure whether that's the way she wants her life to go.

Caspian Blackwell is enjoying life as a newlywed in Edinburgh - although in his heart, he's missing living in Devon. A spate of redundancies at work has him pondering his future - but he worries his new wife's heart is engaged elsewhere when she becomes increasingly distant.

Can sun, sea and sand send the two couples back into

more harmonious waters?

Healing The Heartbreak

Isla Blackwell thought she knew what love was.

But when her five year relationship ends in heartbreak, no home, and no job, she decides to take up her cousin's offer of a break in beautiful coastal Devon.

She expects sea, sand and perhaps some confort for her shattered soul - but when she starts taking shifts at a local bookshop, could love be on the cards?

With the guidance of her cousin Caspian and the rest of his family, as well as the handsome Luca, can Isla heal her broken heart?

'Healing the Heartbreak' is Book Seven in 'The South West Series', but can be read as a standalone novel.

BOOKS BY THIS AUTHOR

The Love Of A Lord

When grieving hearts find each other, can love overcome secrets, vows and society's expectations?

Compelled to uncover the secret surrounding her mother's death, Annelise Edwards unexpectedly finds herself the guest of the handsome Lord Gifford.

Lord Nicholas Gifford has no interest in women after being jilted by his betrothed, but he cannot ignore his sense of duty when a mysterious woman appears on his doorstep during a terrible storm and falls ill.

As they wait for the storm and Annelise's fever to pass, they are forced to share the grief that is weighing on both their hearts. And when Nicholas becomes more involved in Annelise's efforts to piece together her mother's past, it becomes increasingly difficult to deny their blooming attraction.

Will Nicholas give up the lonely life he has become accustomed to? And will it even matter once he finds out Annelise's mother was nothing but their maid?

If you like your rags to riches romance mixed with Tudor drama, you'll love this heart-warming first novel in the touching The Hearts of Tudor England series.

The Love of a Lord is book one in The Hearts of Tudor England series, and can be read as a standalone novel.

Can't Let My Heart Fall

When a marriage is arranged for Alice and Christopher, love was never part of the bargain.

Alice Page long ago swore she would never fall in love. After watching her father's heartbreak at the death of her mother, and Queen Katherine's pain at her husband's philandering, it just doesn't seem worth the pain.

Marriage to Christopher Danley, however, makes keeping that solemn vow to herself somewhat difficult. In the daytime she can keep her distance, but at night she realises she has never felt closer to another human before.

Lord Christopher 'Kit' Danley knows he will be an Earl one day, but he plans to spend every moment of the time before that happens travelling the seas and discovering new lands. When his father delivers an ultimatum, marriage is the only option – but never did he imagine he would find marriage as enjoyable as he does with Lady Alice.

With Alice panicking at realising her heart may be lost

to the handsome Kit Danley, and Kit called away on the King's business, can love flourish in this marriage of convenience?

Can't Let My Heart Fall is book two in The Hearts of Tudor England series, and can be read as a standalone novel.

Misrule My Heart

When Isabel realises over the Twelve Days of Christmas that she cannot marry the man she is required to, will she follow her family's wishes or her heart's desires?

Isabel Radcliffe knows she must marry well. As the daughter of a merchant who has risen at court, many opportunities are within her grasp - and marrying a Lord is one of them.

When her father hosts nobility over the Twelve Days of Christmas, she knows she will meet the man he wishes her to marry, and begin the life that has been laid out before her.

What she does not expect is for him to be quite so old or quite so unpleasant...

Suddenly, the duty binding her to such a life-changing decision feels like too much of a sacrifice. And when her head and heart are turned by the dashing and daring stable lad Avery, she questions whether she can follow through with her father's wishes.

A tale of love, duty and the magic of Christmas, with a

dose of Tudor drama.

Misrule My Heart is book three in 'The Hearts of Tudor England' series, and can be read as a standalone novel.

Saving Grace's Heart

Since witnessing her sister's romantic elopement, Grace Radcliffe has been determined to choose her own husband.

And while finding excuses not to marry every man her father has put in her path has worked so far, she knows time is not on her side - and so she sets her sights on the handsome Duke of Lincoln, planning to ensure they are a good match before letting her father seal the deal.

When Harry, the dashing new Duke of Leicester, is put in her path instead, she knows there must be something wrong with him - for her father has never picked well in the past.

But when he helps her in her hour of greatest need, she begins to question that judgement.

Can Grace find the route to true love? Or will her free-spirited ways lead her into a loveless marriage?

Saving Grace's Heart is Book Four in 'The Hearts of Tudor England' Series, and can be read as a standalone novel.

Learning To Love Once More

A widowed Earl, a lonely governess, and a whole lot of heartbreak.

James, Earl of Tetbury, has never known an all-consuming love - but after losing his wife to the perils of childbirth, he resolved not to suffer that pain again.

Fed up of being a burden on her Aunt and Uncle, orphaned Catherine Thompkins decides being a governess will fill the loneliness in her soul and provide her with a modicum of independence. What she is not expecting is to fall in love with the Earl she is working for.

When James realises he and the children need Catherine in order to flourish, he offers marriage - but in name only. There will be no more children, he is resolute about that.

As Catherine falls deeper and deeper in love with the damaged Earl, can she persuade him that love is worth risking your heart for?

Learning to Love Once More is Book Five in 'The Hearts of Tudor England' series, and can be read as a standalone novel.

An Innocent Heart

On the same day as Henry VIII's second daughter is born, Elizabeth Beaufort makes her way into the world. Inspired by the way the Princess lives her life, she vows to live as a maid - no love, no marriage, no children.

But as the Tudor dynasty sends lives in England reeling,

can Bessie Beaufort's heart remain caged?

Edward Ferrers has always known he will marry and carry on his father's merchant business. In fact, such a marriage has been lined up for him for several years - until a chance meeting at the Tudor Court sends his heart racing for Bessie Beaufort.

In a time of courtly love, female purity and religious upset, can Edward persuade Bessie that their love is worth fighting for?

An Innocent Heart is Book Six in 'The Hearts of Tudor England' series, and can be read as a standalone novel.

Let Love Grow

Lady Lily Merriweather has waited a long time for love to blossom. Through the death of her father, the loss of their fortune and their relocation to Bath, she has held steadfast in the opinion that true love will be found. Can she find it right beneath her nose?

Hugh Baxter was rather irritated when his father asked him to keep an eye on his deceased best friend's daughters. But Lady Lily soon becomes a close friend and ally, especially during the Bath season - a dangerous time for any unwed man.

In the elegance and glamour of the season, will Lily and Hugh realise that their feelings for one another are more than platonic?

Printed in Great Britain
by Amazon